NAMES: Roland S Brown/Rahim Tracey (**Editor**)

TEL: **876** 845-3738

POSTAL CODE: JMDCN17

ADDRESS: Gayle Town District, Borobridge P.O., St. Ann

PREVIOUS WRITING EXPERIENCE: No publish work

WORD COUNT: 31095

SPECIAL THANKS: The Gayle Town(G-Town) family thanks for the support. Tresann, Dena, Rushae, Tickaya, Pinkie, Auntie Rose, Mr Dalley, Mr Sheldon Bailey, Mr Chang, Miss Jarrett, Miss Mack, Sister Julie, Bev, Risca, Sedricka, Crissy, Leedy, Cretine, Judi,Mr Cross, Miss Heather Morgan (NCB), Pheobe, Norma, Teneisha, Dougie, Seddy, Barb, Skull,Terro, Second Son Of God, Cam, Redz, Dj Blacks, Cory, Azy, Bunny, Rosie, Nicko, Shaq The World, Die-nesty, Kazzy, Headless, Vizier, Grato, Tallis, Sab, Jenelle, Bling, Dope Slug, Balla Shaun, Alien Tek, Jovene, Barry, Tall Tree, Raza, Uncle Earlie, Rax, Pam, Steel, Miss Brown, Dan Dan, Daniel. Thanks to my mom Phyllysia Gaynor my father Howard Brown and my aunt Aunty Dell, Ordeen my sister, Fabian my brother respect to Natty as well. Seal it wid patwa big up oonu self everybody weh support mi work. Thanks to everyone for supporting my work.

Movie Script/Book: Fiery Eye Beast

Table of Contents

Pages

Introduction

1

Synopis

3

Motives Behind Our Cruel Deeds

6

Butcher Karma: The Butcher Who Get Butcher

6

Karma The Trench That Blood Follow

10

The Fiery Eye Beast: Rolling Calf

13

Curse Bloodline: Demon Slayers

21

Tides of Flames: Who Will Row the Boat to Hell?

29

Redemption: Good to Be Bad and Bad to Be Good

39

Additional Motivational Information

44

INTRODUCTION

The Rolling Calf or Roaring Calf is a mythical creature in the Jamaica story telling classic. It's classify with spirit or undead with what Jamaican people refer to as duppy. Stories of the mythical creature is past on from older individuals in society to children especially if they misbehave. The Rolling Calf story tell of a dishonest person who die and reborn as the creature, folklore often speak of a butcher the Rolling Calf is believe to be male. The Roaring Calf have superstitious powers it can transform into various animals the myth describe a white and black goat with spots as a deadly creature. The most powerful is the brindle cat, this myth bring fear Jamaicans believe crossing path with a cat at certain time is bad luck. The myth describe the creature as a huge cow having red blood eyes and a clanking chain that drag and make a terrifying noise. Story tellers also give the creature characteristics of releasing fire and smoke from its nostrils, the story tell of the toxic outburst that the Rolling Calf use when a victim is under the moon. In Jamaica kids are afraid of location of cotton trees and bamboos in the mythical world place like that is home for the Rolling Calf in the day.

The myth encourage the mind to believe the Rolling Calf is a devil spirit in the form of an animal, the Roaring Calf roams at nights mostly in cane season molasses is something it desire. Story tell of the Rolling Calf lying in the road blocking a person path . The myth method of dealing with the Rolling Calf is using a tarred whip in the left hand to flog the creature, the creature is also pusillanimous when it come to the moon. The myth state that when the Rolling Calf attack night time travellers with wicked intentions. A person can escape by dropping objects and count or run to intersection this is believe to confuse the creature. There is also a next method of sticking a knife in the ground the creature will stop chasing the victim, Jamaican expletives can also ward off the Rolling Calf. Individuals believe in other methods like using an old piece of iron or enormous object to make lot of loud noise to escape the creature wicked intentions. The dreadful story brings hellish beliefs that people who claim to see the creature is fill with fear and their head start swelling instantly. The Rolling Calf is also fearful of dogs; the story mentions the Rolling Calf retreating lot of times due to its cynophobic qualities. The story develop when the British invade Jamaica, the story state slaves bury treasures and follow the treasure, their masters deeds once they complete their tasks. The stories never fail to mention curse place that is haunt by creatures. Obeah and myths are Jamaican traditions that will not die easily, if a cotton tree is cut down rum must be pour and animal blood spill. There is a term for individuals that chant and talk of the future, locals call them warner man. This practice still take place in modern times when a house is being construct. This serve to show the spirit respect to ensure the person or persons safety. In mythical tradition people prefer travelling in moonlight since the Rolling Calf is afraid of the moon. Methods of warding off the calf as mythical tradition describe cutting ten and making signs ten times with a knife. This will let the creature surround its victims ten times giving them chance to escape.

Deadly abilities in the myth about the Rolling Calf is that it can blow bad breath upon you, if you manage to frighten the beast away leave the spot before it return. To avoid the the Rolling Calf according to myth avoiding rural areas can keep the Rolling Calf away, the myth never mention the fiery eye beast attacking cities, mostly country folks relate to the myth. The reason for more fear when mentioning the myth is that there was lack of light sources; the night contain mostly darkness before electricity was invent. Street lamps were not an option; people use bottle torch or in Jamaican term lundie this item is known in other part of the world as torch. Rolling Calf are mostly describe as being dangerous since they are believe to be butchers, who give short weight who resurrect when they die. The fiery eye beast is also describe as having black and white spots with blazing red eyes, the back feet are those of goat the front consist of one human and a horse hoof. It has a collar around its neck with a chain that attach which drag along its neck, the myth claim that Satan give the beast the chains to warn people of its approach. Rituals of trying to ward off the Rolling Calf in the mythical world, a ritual is to dig a hole and bury a cotton ball pour rum over the area and light it, this will stop the creature, from doing any harm. If the person performing the ritual blood get mix with the rum this can contaminate the ritual. This will haunt the performer of the ritual haunt him with nightmares and drive him mad to kill himself. In modern Jamaica if you ask anyone over the age of 50 about Rolling Calf, they might try to deny the myth but in their mind they hear stories about someone the creature attack. Many think the Rolling Calf is create out of fear and tradition base on our

Jamaicans African heritage which is fill with witchcraft and strong beliefs in superstitions, the culture was transfer orally from generations to generations. These stories of to be transfer by good story tellers, the myth claim to be more terrifying when an ancestor past on the traditions at night-time, this practice rarely happen in modern Jamaica. The story of the Rolling Calf lives on whether its myth or not mentioning the Rolling Calf ring a bell when talking to a Jamaican.

SYNOPSIS: **The Fiery Eye Beast**

THE FIERY EYE BEAST (26.04.19)   Author Name: Roland S. Brown. LOGLINE: A fierce demonic fiery eye beast with chains haunt a local Jamaican village.   Characters include: Hades King- A retire US Navy Seal who hunt down the demon base on hearings that the demon kill his belove daughter Adrienna. He serve in the Persian Gulf War, his MO is to find happiness after his retirement, life have other plans for him.   Rollin Taur - A hunter who is train in SDA (Special Demon Academy) and study ancient demonologies. He is a member of a family that suffer a dark curse he must travel perilous roads to decide his destiny. The others include: The butcher(member of the curse bloodline, founder of Rollin Taur destiny), butcher wife, butcher daughter, Police Superintendent, 9 Police Officers, Snow partner in crime(Snow henchman), the cursing lady (the lady who hate the butcher with a passion), Police officer brother(a officer brother who die in a tragic accident), little boy with the cursing lady(a little boy who Rollin Taur recognize from a photo, the kid is a member of the curse bloodline; the little kid hate the butcher even though the butcher care about him), Mrs Munez(Pastor Munez wife), Pastor Munez kids(the kids who stare at Okill when he visit Pastor Munez the kids father), Psycho(maniac member of vilage enforcers he share a secret with the butcher), David(crime kingpin, businessman and millionaire), David(crime king pin, business man, self acclaim village enforcer leader), bartender(Sapphire Peach hustle associate), Sapphire Peach(undercover stripper), Pastor Munez(Minister Of Religion), Cadence(11 year old kid Snow daughter), Charity(teenage girl), Zacky(teenage boy) ,Okill(Convict), Snow(drugs overlord) ,Zioness Taur(Rollin Taur daughter), Cuceritor Invige Taur(Rollin Taur son), Warner man(A powerful man who chant prophecies),Mass Tahta(Jamaican man),Tall rough looking man at the bar(A regular who visit the bar), drunk sleeping man(a drunkard who sleep in the bar at times), the strange looking man(an individual who is a passer by) old woman with shrieking voice(a rebel old lady that complain about her husband missing animals), criminals(Local criminals who steal the village people animal), Downie(retard who stand at the bar door as an activity), Scyte(Zioness Salvation demon hunter dog). Doctor Zioness Salvation- Phd in demonology and ancient Egyptian hieroglyphics also study at SDA. She is Rolling Taur ex and best friend. George- Senile elder who always talk stories about the fiery eyes beast. He makes a pact with the devil but betray the devil, after too much evil deeds doing good is a method he hopes to use and find salvation. Synopsis: A lady in a burning building chanting strange languages her face display terror, a man with a shotgun start shooting at a ball of fire, loud clanking chains terrorize the man. The man continues shooting and large ball of fire approach him from various directions.

Motives Behind Our Cruel Deeds (06.06.66).

There was a certain tale in the land of wood and water. This gruesome tale become a tradition that let the heart dance when fear plays the music. In a local village the people were accustom to living in peace and harmony, subsistence economy was like gold to the local folks. Where there is occurrence of good deeds, have expectations that there might be bad deeds. In the same way one cannot have peace without war, a person cannot expect good deeds and happiness without terrible actions. A butcher live on the hillside away from the small village with his humble loving family. He was a kind man and everyone was his friend except poverty with hunger. He stays on the hillside lot of times and let food reach a few local folks plate. With the gentle kind heart he has, if he was bless with the power to let food fall from the sky, hunger would pack a bag and leave his village. Below his home in the village the people feel poverty breathing down their neck on a daily basis. The villagers inhale hunger it was their oxygen living was happiness their carbon dioxide was struggles that never go far. Hunger knock on the doors at times not neighbours. They unwilling shake hands with hunger at times and look in all directions if poverty is approaching. The cane season was the villagers last option for hope. They wish the cane season would bring sweetness, and let bitterness exit the village. Survival of the fittest the part of our nature that we utilize without realizing. Natural disasters attack the village with cruelty, flood destroy most of their crops, a few months after the tropics face a terrible drought. The villagers only hope was if they find a bit of crop since cane season was approaching. The animals that local folks rear start get missing there was a rumour, that missing animals were kill and sell in the capital it was a big business. Few months of animals disappearance take place the men become angry and display cruelty; just passing someone property could get you kill or chop to death. Animals get missing on a daily basis for months, this develop in lot of lies and local false investigations by local folks. On a dark lonely night two men dress in masks with guns drive a car and take up some animal. The small village only have one entrance the exit was over a steep hill nickname Mullet Gully by local folks.

    A man coming from the bar notice the strange car without hesitation he blows a whistle. This was a method which take place in private by local village enforcers in the villagers sight; a militant group of men with cutlass no age limit. Serious wild and dangerous the qualities you need to become a member. The whistle echo across the small village and it come to life slowly but surely like a football match that turn out for the better. The thieves become alarm and lack of plans confuse them. They where close to the steep hill at the end of the village to escape fast driving was the best option on the table. The driver speeds off he drives for a few minutes until he passes a deep corner and approach a stretch border by a hillside. The driver speed harder for a few seconds follow by a thud, the loud pandemonium in the night echo throughout the village, the roosters might lose their duty. A large boulder hit the side of the car fright fear and the impact from the boulder, let the driver lose control. The driver finds his car trying to have a relationship with a big tall tree love let both lovers crumble. The tree falls down; the car collision leaves the car damage. The driver was unconscious, the other criminal was injure badly as well. The wild whistling whistle willing send signals. One of the criminal struggle to open the door, it was painful broken glass pierce his hand he tries to feel and take some of the splinters from his injuries. He smells danger and see escaping as the most reasonable solution. He manages to get out through the car window. The driver sits there hardly moving, "come on partner let's move" the man outside speak in a painful tone. A whistle blows close to him in the nearby bushes, he takes out his gun and point. Without hesitating fear show his wisdom which is shadow by cowardice he uses his remaining strength to attempt escape. Six men approach the car first with caution, another six appear from the opposite direction. They inspect the car drag out the driver injure body, next signal with a whistle six more men appear. The unconscious driver begins to gain a bit of consciousness through his almost closing eyes, he glimpses shine objects in few of the men hands. A tall rough looking man appear, he has a fork in his hand one of the teeth from the fork was missing, his hat was stylish the design let it look like the man have two horns. The crowd from the small village appear. "Where is the criminal that let my animals get missing like my front teeth, I want a piece of him." "I know my husband is old but the old horse could fire up the track a few more times, they steal our animals let him stress." "Now what's in his pants is dead and bury, just waiting for the rest of him to die" it was a fine shrieking voice from an old lady.

The village enforcer leader check the vehicle take out the animals ask one of his subordinate to return the animals to the rightful owner. "See my people the devil prey on the meek, let us send him a message in blood so he knoweth the wrath of God" he looks around. "No kids are here right?" The beast inside the angry suffering individuals from the village need to quench its thirst with blood. "Give me piece of him please" the old lady talks in a trembling voice. They make way the criminal beg but it was in vain she did not care about his words. She gives the crowd an old wicked witch stare goes over the criminal. "Please don't do it I was force to do this" he sounds as he uses his last breath to beg for his life. He holds up his hand but the sharp machete cut through his hand fly to a next destination and leave a deep red trench in his forehead. She gives him multiple chops the second chop has already point the criminal toward mr death direction. Hey!! Hey!! She hears a few command after from the village leader enforcer. She starts crying and walk with blood all over her attire she left the crowd and put out the rest of her anger on a tree until the small tree fall. The dead body on the ground was important the people turn to a swarm of angry wasps. They start circling and chopping the body, throwing big stones and other dangerous weapons they create for this specific mission. After they finish a mongrel take one of the hand and run off. "What the.... hell?" The village leader hiss his teeth give a grim smile next in a loud voice he says "enjoy mongrel thanks for helping give the vultures and ants the message free food is available." He searches the car after find a machete with initials on it he looks around in the crowd. The eighteen village enforcers stay behind while everyone else leave, the blood that run in the small trench in the earth from the body was trample. The community enforcer leader and his village enforcers walk toward the hill in the dark without lights, only the sharpness of their weapons glisten in the in the night.

Butcher Karma: The Butcher Who

Get Butcher

The butcher was unaware of the cruelty that was taking place in the night. He decides to go to town late in the night to try and get a new machete and his favourite molasses. He walks to town just for molasses at times but cynophobia prevent him from going to town more often. "Who is the biggest fool alive?" He thinks for a few seconds. "Me... why did i even guess that." "I lend a stranger my favourite machete three days ago because he tells me a sad story." "Now he probably in his bed comfortable laughing after me." "Well on the bright side I will find the love of my life molasses, hope those mangy stinking mongrel don't rush me." It come across his mind as a 12-year-old kid a dog bite him on his buttocks. That drag him through high school as a mockery for kids, he even gets a nickname even as a grown up he hate that name. "A biter I lose my girl over that nickname stupid I could have been famous that nickname hold back my potentials" he curses himself with his nickname from high school. The butcher hear rustling and his heart feel like it was beating fast in his mouth. Suddenly a goat with black and white spots jump out the bush and gallop across the road. The butcher stays silent for awhile and listen he wonder if it was a goat killer dog chasing the animal. He hears a louder rustle he stops and listen. He hears the rustle again in the nearby bushes, he stops for a moment and listen cautiously. He hears the rustle come from a direction behind him, he makes baby steps toward the rustle. In the dark under the bright moonlight he glimpses what seems to be a shoes. He did not drop his guard he takes out a knife he was carrying for protection. He walks up to the tree and see a man lying, the distance he was at did not allow him to clearly understand the situation. He disguises his knife and walk faster "Hey what are you doing here, if i may ask???" he attempt to make his question courteous. Help me!! Only his closeness gives him the privilege to hear the tiny desperate voice. He gets closer and realize spin over the person his hands start to soak, by this time the stench from the blood start greeting his nose. Oh no!! He recognizes the face its the same stranger he lends his machete few days ago. He punches the injury man in his face a few times in his mind. Only his kind heart let him resist from punching the injury man in the face, he was the reason he is here alone in the dark figuring how to help a helpless person. A man of his strength and bulit the task was manageable plus the anger deliver motivation. He might have a few words he wants to tell this injury stranger personally.

Home was not a far distance away the struggle that he endures over the years feel like it decides to live on his shoulder. He takes up the dead weight wait steady few seconds to get good balance while grunting was like a sound that deliver motivation; he grunts similar to the animals he butcher. After a journey with fair amount of struggle; he could see his humble little home, the moonlight was bright and he see light from a lamp shining through the window. He fastens his pace he walks up to the door in a struggling loud voice he calls for help. His wife answers in a trembling timid voice "yeeaahh we have company." "Drop him" a voice command from behind him. He could feel a small burn on his neck, by the time a hand swiftly moves across his eyes and hold a knife at his throat "Follow my lead butcher if you hope to live, now put him down slowly." The butcher reluctantly follows his command "Open the door mission accomplish chief" he talk in a brave confident voice. "Where are the other warriors?" A thunderous voice that echo in the dark question the man outside. "We are here chief the situation is cover" a few rough voice men talk one after the other. "Good warriors" he nods two men with him inside hold the butcher wife and daughter more vicious in case a threat exists outside. He disguises his weapon behind him and use the other hand to open the door. The situation was handle the butcher was in a dangerous place. "How long butcher, how long?" "Wwhhaat....are you talking about..." before the butcher finish the statement a piece of stick blackout his mind. The village enforcer leader grabs a tall retard looking man. He shouts furiously "Psycho, if you ever do something without my orders I kill you, my first method of choice is enhancing questioning" he gives Psycho a grave look. "Even you will understand this I will rip up your body parts and feed my little mongrel friend." In the moonlight he has a dangerous dark dreadful deadly destructive appearance. Psycho walk away with some low mumbling. All these actions where well plan, the criminal outside hang up on a big cotton tree, like animals on display at the butcher shop. They carry the butcher unconscious body outside; they use chains to tie him to the big cotton tree that the criminal body hang loosely clothes soak heavily with blood. A man in the crowd ask "David should we give him Italian pepper sausage as well, we pepper that criminal pecker and let him eat it" he start laughing showing his maniac side. "Where is Psycho?" The community leader asks in a loud frighten voice. He remembers the ladies were tie to chair and only one person was watching. You!! You!! He signals to his comrades with pointing fingers. He calls a few warriors "let's check the house" he walks while executing his statement.

He gives the door a hard kick. He sees Psycho assaulting a head, the daughter was alive so David figure it was the butcher wife. He stares in astonishment if he was a weak man he would be on his knees. The other warriors enter the house when they see David stop and stare for a few seconds. Psycho pull up his pants and look around grinning "I ask first David she say she will never go to my level see her head is right at my feet, this is bigger than you all I want her to bring my son." "She fight me so I of to kill her." Butcher wife Psycho price, get my revenge whether it's wrong or right" he sings in an off tune melody. He makes weird movements seems a cargo of craziness land on him. "Dont worry I send that stupid young warrior away he did not see we can fix this I can fix this" he laughs louder. David hold down his head "Ok Psycho finish your craziness." "Yeeeesss bosssss, whoooieee!! "Psycho is one lucky man, bloody butcher daughter and wife one night karma you are next." He gets to action to assault the daughter that was tie on the chair, David run his three teeth fork through Psycho, blood splash all over the butcher daughter. "No more raping, just finish it am not going to jail" he utilizes the common cliché follow by orders to his enforcers with signals. The butcher daughter sees a knife on the ground, David was close by she grabs the knife in a flash. Being an alert person he hears shouting from his comrades, he did not spin around he moves at first. She manages to inflict a stab on his leg. He cries in agony without hesitation he takes the long sharp knife and stab her in the head. She looks in his eyes for a few seconds until she loses her sight. He cut a piece of cloth and wrap his wound, it was bleeding heavily. He goes outside and set his plans in motions, the butcher begin to regain his consciousness. "Am sorry my friend, no time for enhance questioning, we are your judge, jury and executioner." He walks up to the butcher tear off a piece of his shirt, "spread the gasoline" he shouts. "Am sending you off with a smoke my friend you are good person things just get ugly here." "My witch grandma tells me long ago I must kill with cruelty, don't want your ghost haunting me if I live for long." "One of my scout hide and see you concealing animals for a man we murder earlier." "Your wife and daughter tell me you don't know the man, it's a pity we cannot try you and both Delilah tonight at our meeting." "This may be the worst decision I ever make and

I am more on the side that am dead wrong." "Its me or you butcher and
am not going to jail I dream am a rich rich man in the future" he looks in
the butcher eyes as if he wants to see a sign of forgiveness.

        The butcher could not reply the other men cut out his tongue and
tie his mouth with cloth blood soak the cloth. He only makes muffle
sounds and look at David like a lamb to the slaughter while whimpering.
He takes a container with gasoline and soak the butcher clothes. He walks
away limping, a warrior walks up to the butcher cut off a piece of cloth
from the butcher shirt. He forces the cloth through a small opening of the
previous cloth that tie the butcher mouth, hang piece out and apply
flames. He makes quick movements shouting "there is your smoke
butcher see you in hell." The fire start moving toward the butcher he was
wrap in chains, the cloth in the butcher mouth become flames of hell it
start blazing; the butcher eyes get red and smoke float through his
nostrils. Fiery pain rocks the butcher tough body, his pain leave muffle
sound, the village warriors stare with no words from the mouth. David
check his pocket watch it was damage and blood was all over it form in
the shape of a calf head when he utilize a torch to check the time it was
3:03 AM he just rub off the blood. He leaves the fire to complete its task
and call the 18 warriors together. "Now terrible things happen here, we
do somethings bad really bad; we track the criminals he has a gun he kills
the butcher family and set the house on fire." "We were so angry we
catch him and our emotions let us ignore enhance questioning."
"Everyone understand" the village enforcer leader shout and look around
for disapproval with a peaceful-war appearance on his face. "This

situation dies here tonight like the butcher, no mentions if its even me kill me." "After we leave here if we even leave ourselves no turning back." The village enforcer leader gives out commands the men pack sticks on the butcher body, at the big cotton tree and set it on flames again. They set the butcher house on fire, it blazes giving the furnace of hell competition. They leave the criminal body on the higher branch which he was hang, this was done to promote heroism. The flames from hell brighten their night as they walk. Everyone walk off the hillside, with bloody hands that water cannot cleanse. Except the butcher he limps off the hillside in pain with hands that water cannot cleanse.

Karma The Trench That Blood Follow (06.06.06)

A swarm of flies devour a small decaying body; the flies start laying maggots as they walk about busily. A truck with materials disturb the flies the swarm scatter and the wheels of the trucks become party crasher. The small decaying body get stuck on the truck wheel. It was cane season everybody was getting busy at the factories and a new building was under construction.

"My pocket watch buck call it luck time, shine like the sunshine, i kkkkkeeep a gold nine" David struggle over his lyrics and start talking with lyrics. "Stop it David stay posi-tive." Uncle David!! Uncle David!! "You Trying to stay young" Zacky mimick the lyrics in a ridiculous manner. "Geez give the old man a break I am practicing from last year summer; music can make you legendary so am willing to give it an old shot" he gives a broad old smile which hide his character. "Ok Uncle David its funny only need a red nose but am not doubting you, C.Y.O.P create your own path." Zacky looks at the millionaire after his statement. Zacky just leave high school and get a job at the construction site, he tries keep it a secret that he gets his classmate pregnant. He decides to take up the responsibility and let his dream of going to bootcamp slide. "So how is work going Zacky Zack?Uncle David look at Zacky he still could see the breast milk on the boy mouth. "Its ok Uncle David thanks for being concern it make a lot of difference" he talks and gaze downward for a few seconds. He uses this opportunity to stare and wonder which of David foot was injury back in the days. Both feet look feeble and appear like they might break if too much pressure get apply. Zacky mind go in a trance like state he gets distract by the old man strong voice. "It's life son its not everytime we see greatness; don't mean we should stop making effort." "I start from shining shoes at a bar, now I can buy that shoes store and bar cash" he tries to avoid bragging in his statement. "Thanks for the motivation Uncle David, you kknnoww I got a girl.... forget it" he searches his mind for a convincing story. "I got a girlfriend you soon meet her" the fake mask on his face almost fall off he employ a fake chuckle. "Ok Zacky you have a girlfriend or girlfriend friend?" he starts laughing. "Okay son let's go have a drink at the snack stand you are 18??" Right Zacky????? He looks at Zacky and smile after his questions. Zacky change the mood "let me rap now, Friday when I check I want my cheque, am about cash I want to cash, I like to count so let that count" he shows his musical skills to the elder. "Okay you have Talent two Zack let's do an album I will handle the expense" he searches for Zacky reactions toward his business proposal. Zacky just laugh at the nickname two Zack. "Am no rapper i know, i want to build a studio after this project, I might get inspire and do a few bars, see it its sweet like chocolate" David talk and move his hands like he is imitating a new school gangster. "So you got style I see Uncle David; I will call you candy bar or chocolate; so sweet everyone laughs when you wrap up yourself." They walk off down the road talking and having a bit of joy from laughter for the moment like high schoolers.

They were interrupt by a powerful male voice. Esau!! Esau!! "Trouble grasp the heel!!" Esauuu!! The voice was coming from a corner close by, Zacky look in disbelief when the man appear he was dress in red and black clothing matching turban around his head. A big black flag with ancient symbols written in crimson red all over, he waves the flag rapidly. He stops at David feet look him directly in the eyes walk past, return and look in his eyes again. "Esau!! Evil evade evenly everyday everywhere, even evening sins don't evaporate to heaven to get evaluate" he marches around David and Zacky chanting the words. "Can I ask you a question Noah??" David speak while looking at him marching around, chanting loud and looking exhaust. He stops for a few seconds "you just did Mr Aristocratic David" he continues his actions. "When is the great flood coming?" "Will you part the red sea and save us or fall manna from the sky" David talk and stare at him ridiculously. "Get out of here Malachi before I call the Police and let you visit Satan in hell false prophet." The chanting man walk away waving his big red flag and chanting in a manner that let him look psychologically challenge. David and Zacky continue walking, Zacky look at him he tries to conceal it but he sees the wondering what if look in his eyes. "You know I have an older brother he should be controlling the family business but this is life destiny cannot be change" David words sound struggling a bit." He takes out a cigrette and display his age when he trembles a bit to light his cigarette; next take out his phone and start reading without wondering if Zacky have any interest. "You can try steer life all you want but it dont exactly travel in the directions we plan; you in the light and blink for a few seconds and you staring in darkness." "It's life so complaining hardly change anything just have faith and you might see happy times, that's my motivation Zacky what's yours?" He looks Zacky right in the eyes like he was searching his soul and that was the gateway. "Ummmm I don't know, my mother that play the role of a father" he gives a nervous chuckle with his statement. They arrive at the snack stop "Sapphire Peeeach, Mr Dick your best friend is here" David powerful voice alert Sapphire Peach David and Zacky both start laughing. "Mr Dick the small one or big one in your case old man the dead one" she talks in a sexy singing tone. Zacky was amaze at Uncle David adaptive emotions he seems like the type that could just walk out of hell and look like he spends years in heaven. Sapphire would of to be a genius to know his day was not going as he plan. "Two drink for me and the potential millionaire" he smiles at Zacky. "Don't you look a bit too young to be dri...." she was interrupt by Uncle David sum of money. "Buy yourself a drink keep the change Sapphire" he displays a bit of graveness in his voice. "Let's have fun then boys, I have a riddle if my tongue crawl on you like a caterpillar which creature will you see" she laughs while she asks. "Give me a pack of cigadeath, my last one is going to hell now" David beat the cigarette in an inverse position before burning it with flames. "No cigarettes for you old perve answer my question" she talks jokingly David just continue burning the cigarette. "Firefly you kinda old geeza you con me last month I wait under the same big cotton; the same one I cut down to start my business" David sound serious and a bit disrespectful. "I follow your instructions wait there in the dark with the protection on my half dead third leg, no sign of you Sapphire am old more possibility of me dying increase." "Let me die on the glorious land between your legs." "Hold up old man, you already dead no cemetery here so you can finish dying go somewhere else" Sapphire start the laughing she was like a laughing detonator because she triggers off David and Zacky.The old man laugh, drops to the ground and ask Zacky for help who was extra weak from energy decreasing laughter. At times he takes off his weird looking hat that look like it have horns and spin around it and dance when the jokes get intense. The fun calm down for awhile "there is a new girl at my bar, I hear she blow flute sssshh let's call her Piper" she winks at Zacky and David. "Dont get hypnotize by her music, she might use it to lead you right to hell on earth here with your wife" she starts laughing louder. David start ordering more liquor. "So....." David stare directly in her eyes without finishing his sentence. "Price??" David looks at her serious and act like she was a stranger doing business with him. "Let me... think about... it" Sapphire Peach give a slight wink after she finish counting her words. David start laugjing again "no interest you are the nun I want to raise the dead again now that would be holy, I will let you scream in agony before I die on you" David laugh and talk like a young male. "Woow!! "Magic the dead is talking brave nowadays oh just remember its just part of you dead" Sapphire Peach start laughing again. "Check the morgue might find your type down there" Boooom!! The whole place goes in silence for a few seconds.

The dogs in the surrounding start howling, the dogs were barking earlier a large group of vultures circle the sky from early in the morning. "Maybe they just blasting rocks" David talk in an unsure voice. After a few minutes some vehicle start speeding off to the opposite directions one was coming toward David. The vehicle stops at the snack stand a man hop out "bad news Mr David the explosion seems to kill 18 people that the men discover so far; there are more injuries some might be cover under debris" he sounds nervous. "Where is my tone, Jacky stay" Uncle David was too shock to recognize his error. They rush with sorrow toward the horrific site blood, flesh agonizing crying was everywhere it feels like an idea of judgement day. David could feel the weight coming down on his shoulder. He notices an emerald ring in a small pool of blood, he drops to his knees and start crying a part of him no one never see. It was his best friend ring he buy him that ring, they both share a secret the man has cancer and doctor give him a few months. His family abandon him David would pay for the funeral willingly; the man was a man with pride he still wants to help David in his weaken state. The horrific raging incident, bring with it howling sound and fierce emotions as the residents look up at the peaceful sky and wonder if they will get an explanation. The peaceful sky gets angry and bring hard rain to cleanse away the sins and blood. Large puddles of blood and water fill the gopher holes, one of them form out in a calf like creature head. The dark night falls and assist sorrow to wrap up the people of the village in discomfort. The whole village get silence and only muttering make contact with the ears no loud music the village fight for life until suffocation get the best of it.

The Fiery Eye Beast (Rolling Calf)

Okill was happy to see the outside world he spends 10 years in prison. The first person he hopes to see was Adrienna he has quite a few question. He wonders if she gets a husband and kids that steal her beauty. "Okill??" He could hear the excitement in her voice he hesitates for awhile, to conceal his own excitement. "The music that make me soar to the sky Mozart; your voice is like music to my ear, keep playing am going to close my eyes and picture heaven" he turns around with a big wide smile on his face. "After all this time you greet me with a romantic phrase, even in the dark I could not fall for that, it's good though try it over Sapphire Peach might work" she genuinely smiles before proceeding to the next question. "How are you doing??" "Its being awhile you look good to be coming from prison, I cannot deny that" her automatic mouth fire shot at him rapidly. "Am doing ok just balancing things out, thanks you?" Okill statement and question wins the race but Adrienna statement could see them at the finish line. "Success in our village is replace by deaths, since lately I feel like my spirit is in a cloudy atmosphere trying to escape this place." "David best friend and 17 people were injure down by the new factory, some say a boiling blood of water is in the middle of the road that we walk over everyday and we are curse." "The strange looking man dress in red and black with a flag, he says we must all repent before blood drown the village" she looks both side similar to kids hiding a kid secret from adults. "I hear a few things while I was in the hell hole, I was lock up from society not lock away from society information" he memorizes a few flashbacks of some of things he hears. He remembers how a mysterious lady repel a coffin with six birds floating across the sky, asking for bad credit from the devil pawns. It's prison expect all type of story; he even hears at once that every cane season a ghost have sex with a young lady. The story tells of how a man see a next man abusing an animal; the man offers the man money to keep his mouth. He releases the secret and the man obeah his daughter to suffer a terrible journey. Rumours even spread that the lady pregnant for 12 months and her baby born having a dog appearance. Prison life let you receive rumours as a prisoner just to listen the story shorten your time in the hell hole. Night time begin to stare daytime in the face. "You want to leave the convo until tomorrow??" Okill notice a bit of upset after his statement. "I will find you Adrienna" he says that even though if it was up to him she could stay forever heart, mind bed anywhere she chooses. "No its fine with me, you not eye raping me like a convict down at the factory, unless you want space to go see

Sapphire Peach "she says the last part of her sentence in a cheerful singing voice. "She and her damn caterpillars lines th...." A car pulls up and honk, the window goes half way down a big smile display in the dark. "I see Romeo find Juliet that's great another love story, anytime you feel like a convict give me a call" Sapphire Peach wink at Okill. He could not help but laugh Adrienna give him an angry look. "Move on Peach take your business with Okill in your territory if you not too busy" Adrienna was getting a bit angry. "Shush hating dove this chicken head will get feeding anyway she please, it was nice seeing you hope you are ok enjoy your day Adrienna" Sapphire drive away laughing like an actor trying to play an evil role in a movie. Okill and Adrienna continue walking and talking. "This is my stop O" she stop close to a big cotton tree. "My husband and kids must be worrying by now, I will see you around town" she looks Okill directly in the eyes and see a doubtful look. No words for two minutes between them, she smiles while looking into Okill eyes and see the coldness that hope for warmth. "You know am joking right, I dont find anyone worthy as yet" she starts chuckling. "You getting soft Okill, the heart is made of flesh but it can be tough as a stone you choose" she tries to sound like her father. "By the way he retires from the Navy Seal for now I guess, he coming home soon" Adrienna speak with average excitement. Okill find a bit of fun in the situation he gives the that's not too funny to me chuckle. Its good for the soul, only suspense he has over the year is wonder if the warden have lot of strength behind the baton. If baton beating challenge was a test he would get a job right out of prison, especially since his resume is right above his eyes a two-inch scar. During this moment he wonder if he should try kissing Adrienna, just to analyze her feelings for him. In his sight just knowing someone like her is a win for him.

A different feelings confront Okill it was a different type of coldness follow by strange heat. Adrienna was talking but Okill head start swelling he hardly hear her voice. He notices a flicker of red light coming from the big gigantic cotton tree. He takes his eyes off for a few seconds, he looks back in the same location. Two red blazing eyes appear; he points toward the location because words get tangle in his vocal box. "Hey you still there" she was clueless to what Okill sight engage. The fiery eyes move at full speed from the big cotton tree root, the dark make it impossible for positive description. The fiery ball of fire charge at fast pace and attack Adrienna first the force leaves an impact on Okill, his body fly mid air and he land on some grass. Okill could hear the clanking of chains which instill fear and paralyze his whole body with fear. He finally regains some sense he feels his pocket for a pen knife he buy in the supermarket. He strikes his light in the dark and stare at hell itself, he sees two humongous eyes the colour of fire with the shape of a cow smoke and fire exhale from the calf like creature nostrils. The calf like creature has black and white spots all over. It starts moving closer to Okill he strike the light and get a quick glimpse of Adrienna her white blouse turn valentine colour. He knows escaping from this situation was the best option even if it was a dream. He hears the unnerving clanking of chains but he did not look back. He run trip and drop in the dark his hands groping as if he was searching for a valuable object he lost. He could feel the toxic breath breathing down his neck, while running the pen knife drop from him and stick up in the ground. He run toward the crossroads the clanking of the chain turns to an opposite direction. He run until his body decide it need rest. A millions thoughts fill Okill head first day out and a body was on the ground and he was there, plus Sapphire will definitely tell the police Adrienna was with him. If she resists to share information they just of to pay cash no wonder her nickname is the hustler stripper. He checks his clothes no blood was on him that's a good start. He remembers the Reverend house was close by, maybe he can help with the situation. The minister of religion was having a late supper with his family. Okill walk up to the door finger wrap tightly he pounds the door, his confuse step with heavy hardboots in all directions thump the hollow concrete on the steps. Pastor Munez walk to the door he listens cautiously as if the knocking was a rhythm. He feels satisfy after the fourth knocking session. "Who is it?" He tries to sound polite. "Oh God thank God, Pastor Munez is that you? "Am in a lot of trouble pastor hell is right at my heel, I can feel the devil eyes watching me from in the dark" he talks while moving about cowardly he look about in the dark. "Son you just get out of prison what's the matter, you owe money someone chasing you?" He looks at Okill in a confuse way. "Wish it was something like that pastor, wish I was in prison" he breaks down and talk with crying in his voice. "What's the matter son?" "Tell me let me see if i can help" he tries to sound confident but he was getting nervous as well. He wonder if Okill was paranoid from prison or maybe he is high on drugs. "Am no good Pastor but I need you to trust me, Adrienna was kill I was there things happen fast I hardly know what happen" he could not bare holding back those words. "Jesus Christ son we of to go to the station now" he walks inside talk to his wife for a few minutes. He gets his bible and the car keys he could see the worries in his wife eyes when he close the door.

Meanwhile at a bar: David sit there drinking he wish one of his enemies could just be brave and end his life. Someone clears their throat he slowly turns his head to look in that direction. David eyes glimpse the same man dress in red and black with the flag, David walk over to make sure. It was the same man who chant the day before the deaths. He walks toward the man he has a bottle of wine and cup with cubes of ice. "Your prophecy, can I have a drink of righteousness because everything I touch is curse" he talks in a drunking voice. "Jesus you did it again turn water into wine" the stranger with the ridiculous appearance just look at him while he pours out wine. "The Devil children finally get weak, oh God you are mighty you never forsake" he looks upward. David get back to his true form even in his drunken state "let me check the time if I can talk I assume you have answers for me." He goes in his pocket and take out his pocket watch it drops on the table; the pocket watch start spinning on the chains, until the pocket watch face turn toward the ridiculous dressing stranger. The table start vibrating slow next it speed up vibration the bottle of wine falls to the ground splinters scatter everywhere. The stranger body get drag like a truck was pulling lightweight; an unseen force slightly shifts the stool he was sitting on. His eyes turn full white he drops to the ground. He starts spinning saying strange words and froth come from both side of his mouth. "Somebody help" David shout. The stranger get up off the ground he manages to grab a knife from one of the man that come to assist. He seems to be stabbing at himself but it just goes over his shoulder, he tries to slit his throat but the knife turns to the blunt side. He stabs at his belly but he miraculously manages to dodge the cruel attack. David movements let him stumble over a few obstacles before he reach outside just to avoid seeing more blood. The man finally calm down he just acts normal apologize to everyone and give back the owner the knife. He orders a next bottle of wine and tell the waitress to keep the change. Everyone look at him strangely and try to figure what really happen. He moves about swiftly less opportunities for anyone to ask questions. He pours the whole bottle of wine on the ground "this is for the souls of the innocent, vade retro Satana" he walks toward the door briskly. David stay at the door and listen he decide to go home; he walk a bit shaky. He turns back unwillingly when he remembers his phone. Inside the bar was quiet now he decides to still try and get answers. He meets the stranger on the way "stay away from me devil pawn" he looks serious but fear was on his mind. David hear his name mention in the bar and look, when he turns around the stranger was gone, he stares for a few minutes in disbelief, the flapping of wings rapidly disturb the quiet street. He wonders if he drinks too much and go back in the bar to continue drinking.

"Heey David you know I can never know how you manage the un-fortunate loss life present you, I can only have an i-idea" the young lady stumble over a few words. She looks nervous and act like the bar environment was below zero degree celsius, "my father use to say sometime you of to die to live." David look at her with drunken lazy attitude "yeah what a philosopher I bet the devil is glad for his company, I

hear his casket could not open guess he steals from the wrong persons."
David know the young lady father they run a few ganja trafficking
operations few years ago, David have some vital information about the
girl father death he was on the police radar. David and few associates was
out all night camping in the woods, David leave a few seconds later he
hears a shot. He goes back to the camp one of his drunkard friend license
gun misfire and shoot the girl father in the head. The drunkard claim it
was a mistake the police were summon the drunkard get lock up for a few
months before he gets release. The rumour in the street was that the girl
father thief cocaine and cash from the Columbians, contract was on his
head; he was a hard target he gets protection from dirty cops, bribe let
him become a respectful man at the police station. Due to his crime life
his body get treat roughly after awhile it starts decay, funeral day the
family push the casket out of the Church. They claim it was a next man kill
in an extradition in the city, they see the next man in the casket death
announcement in the memorial section. The driver of the hearse that
work at the funeral home of to return the body due to fear of being kill.
The next time they return with police and give the young girl father a
close casket funeral. The young lady and David friendship break apart
from that time. "After the vrooom!!" "Vrooooom Mercedes incident were
I pop your pretty red cherry, never know he was your dad, I even tell him
about the pretty young cherry I was popping" David talk in a solemn
mood which still manage to sound like a younger male bragging about his
player skills. "Poor soul he dies not even knowing I was telling him about
his own daughter, not even know I pay you to keep quiet and abort one of
my seed" David look directly in her eyes while talking. "Why did he trust
an old turkey vulture like me to leave a young slut in my care he leaves

you at my home for two months to go on business" he continues talking. She stays there until teardrops start running from one eye her mouth corner begins to tremble she feel like she could use her bare hands and tear him in two halves. The thoughts of being too nice to show a former friend sympathy for his loss end up affecting s nice person she walks angrily and slam the door exiting the bar. A few minutes later David try to take a short nap. Thud!! A one knock on the door a few seconds after a next thud, follow by a next knock in similar fashion. The whole place goes silent for awhile the music turn off completely after the young lady leave the bar the door was close, with the bar tender and five persons. Three men were labourer at the factory that David own. "Maybe it's that down syndrome boy Downie from across the road doing the same thing" the rough looking tall man walk up to the door while talking. He makes staggering steps since he is a member of the drunkard family. He pulls out a big broad handle knife he continue talking "am going to gut him get rid of his worthless life, next let his mother get a handsome boy from a pedigree like me not a mongrel like his retard father." "Downie!!" He bends down to look and see the same foot but only one this time from the foot he see about six hours ago. The foot remains still for awhile next start stomping the hard dry ground as if it was torment and getting bother. "See the same retard foot but he only shows one" he looks back at the other individuals in the bar when he stands and cast his eyes. He starts bending down again, this time when he looks he see a horse foot and a human foot. He stumbles backward a bit before he attempts to get up. He was about to say something to the other individuals, during that time the fiery eye beast Rolling Calf position on its two front feet, back feet hoist high in the air. A loud thud sound connects to the door. Everyone start screaming one of the rough looking man hand drop on the ground fire was blazing on the hand on the ground. The man start screaming in pain, the whole door fly off after and slam the rough looking man over the counter of the bar, the breaking of glass gives the location of his destination. The loud unnerving clanking of chains being drag on the ground instill deadly fear in the five remaining persons in the bar. The dragging of the chains act like a memo from hell. This action take place in split seconds the bar tender start screaming, the Rolling Calf look around at its victim, the chains around its body drag on the ground. The chains make a fearful terrifying sound, like Satan give it to the Rolling Calf to warn people of its dangerous approach. Everyone start scattering a drunkard that was sleeping in the corner get wake from the horrifying events. He could not talk when he sees the calf like creature with two large eyeballs of fire and smoke coming from the beast nostrils. His tongue feels heavy like lead in his mouth, his body start feeling light, his head start swelling getting ready to explode. His eyes pulp out and his feet could not move. He wonders if he was drunk or if it was a dream. He closes his eyes start counting he regain some movements make a run to the opposite of the fiery danger. He stumbles over a table he slips on an iron chair with the feet up the iron feet chair force through his chest one of the chair inflict damage to his throat as well. The Rolling Calf start rolling in various directions, the horrifying clanking and rattling of the chains paralyze the remaining survivors with fear. David start running toward the door to make an escape the Rolling Calf charge with rage and stuck him on the wall its horn pierce his flesh. The fiery eye beast force him more on the wall and he look right in the large blazing eyes. David start visioning the Rolling Calf pain he vision a sad spirit running and crying, the image appears to be a young runaway slave boy, with chains anchor to his neck. He starts seeing clearer visions dogs start chasing the slave boy and he start limping his feet were sore. Next he visions the butcher with his family and a boy taking payment from Psycho he grins with a evil smile and look at the kid evil when the kid turn his back. David escape the trance and go for a knife with his left hand the knife has initials on some part of the handle. He stabs the Rolling Calf it staggers a few steps back and look David in the eyes. The chains start clanking and it whole body turn fire, it raises its burning chains slowly to David throat and slowly force it in his throat. Next it just wraps the burning chains around his neck and gallop. The Jamaican man from the bar start running and cursing" a judgment day di dehble cum fi wi" he speeds off down the road with the bartender. The next man who did not speak to anyone start running, the Rolling Calf gallop after him, he attempts to run faster when he hears the clanking of the chains. He runs until he charges in a tree and drop flat, he starts having blur visions. He hears the clanking of chains getting closer and the loud sound of fire and smoke coming from the fiery creature nostrils. He lies there patiently anticipating death the fiery eye beast charge toward him at high speed when it gets close it jump over his fearful body. He could feel the sparks of fire burning his face from the fire beast feet. Its feet drops on the ground and make a loud heavy sound. It stares for awhile and exhale toxic breath next gallop in a next direction the man stop his breath for a few seconds. He lies there still and hear the loud heavy chains coming close he eases up his body a bit because his feet were still weak. He looks up and see the two fiery eyes blazing he just close his eyes there was no escaping death. The calf like creature jump over his head and set the road leading toward the bar on fire. The Jamaican man and the bar tender keep running they reach light and start walking, they decide to take the short cut that lead to Pastor Munez home. They walk looking all around sometime bouncing into each other. Their phone lights shine like Police search light looking for criminals. They see a black and white spotted goat in the way, its head was hide by a rock, they hesitate before moving. The bar tender finally decides to make a move because the Jamaican man was behaving reluctant. She draws the rope the white and black goat with spots appear without head, she drop the burning rope speedily. She was hoist in the air by the Rolling Calf, before she drops it hoist her high again and this time she fall over a deep hillside. The Jamaican man run toward the road he exits the short cut the loud clanking of the chains trail him. He run out in the middle of the road and see a bright light, hear the honking of horns, screeching of brakes next his night gets extra dark.

Pastor Munez continue driving he know evil exist and the world is a balance of good and evil. Okill could be getting paranoid and killing people without realizing. After hearing Okill fearful story there was some silence for awhile. "You know the Police will not believe that story son, they will think you are Psycho like psycho from back in the days" he starts talking fast as they go around a corner a goat with black and white spots lie in the road. Pastor Munez look at Okill since he was driving. Okill give his answer by looking in the opposite direction he did not intend to go out there. The road seems lonely and frightful Pastor Munez open his door part way before stepping out. He makes slow steps while looking around, this could have been a decoy for robbers use the animal to stop vehicle. He looks back on Okill who just stare at him in expectations that something might happen. The goat hears the step and start moving toward the bushes. After that they hear a loud sound coming from the bushes on the other side. They hear the trampling, and clanking of chains when it come on the road. Okill pull the car door and run on the road in the dark, Pastor Munez try to call him back it was in vain. Okill drop his old driver licence on the seat. The cow just run on the road and head for the other side of the bush. Pastor Munez get in his van and start driving, he hears the dragging of chains and know it was the same bull. He turns his head to look and make eye to eye contact with two blazing ball of fire. Fright let his trembling hands let go off his steering. His van swerves the bull charge at full speed and slam the moving vehicle, the vehicle crash in a large stone. Pastor Munez start coughing up blood his body was damage badly. The Rolling Calf gallop away for a few metres, draw one of its back feet back and forth until it blaze on fire. Next it charges toward the vehicle and buck it a few times until the front look similar to a crush Pepsi can. The Fiery Eye Beast repeats the actions and fire blaze on its entire body the chains start clanking rapidly. The bull charge at the vehicle and tear it in two halves it leaves the middle of van and rock on fire. The Roaring Calf was successful it sends the dreadful hell message the Rolling Calf leave fire behind it, next proceed on it demonic journey damaging anything in its path.

Zacky check the time it was 3:03 but Charity was feeling lonely and want to see him his home was not far away. He walks at a steady pace in the chilly lonely night. He keeps wondering when both their parents will know that two teenagers were giving them a grand kid in these difficult times. He hears a rustle in the bush he looks but did not see anything. He looks back the sound stop, he continues walking, an old car he past makes a sound like it was being drag, he stops and look back the car shift again. Without hesitating Zacky start running and blowing hard. He hears no sounds but it feels like something was trying to devour him he pushes a board gate and enter Charity home. He starts pounding on the back door, she wakes up quickly and open the door she was expecting him. "What's the matter Zacky, suppose my parents were here?" she shouts the words at him. He was full with fright he just signals at her to stay quiet. She looks in his eyes and decide to follow his command. They lie still there was a low grunting circling the house. The dogs in the yard rush the demonic presence in the yard, there was loud noise and barking. Zacky and Charity hear brawling howl and the tearing down of trees.

Okill!! Okill!! Adrienna voice sounding desperate wake Okill. He wakes up fast and walk to the bathroom he washes his face which feel like it was burning. He smells smoke and notice little red spots in his eyes, he washes the matters from his eyes the spots start getting bigger. He tries to call for help but no words come out of his mouth his feet could not move. Smoke start coming from his nostrils and he feel something painful piercing his forehead. It forces up his flesh slowly he drops to the floor. He feels his forehead and something with a sharp point bore his finger. Blood start running, the pain eases up he look in the glass he sees two short horn and his eyes blazing with fire, each time he exhales it produce toxic breath. He looks at the mirror in disbelief he notices an invert cross on the other side of the wall. He stares and the mirror crack rapidly and a huge Rolling Calf face appear and attack him. Okill wake up with sun shining he was almost naked and somehow he has a chain around his neck. An old lady sees him and call the police they arrest him with ease he was weak from running he could hardly resist. He only tries to prove his innocence by talking. The police take him to the station for questioning they find his knife and identification cards at both of the crime scene.

Curse Bloodline: Demon Slayers

News of the recent event spread through the village, people start leaving and some believe that the village is curse. The passing away of members of the village bring about excruciating pain, even a man consider wicked will have someone who love him. No one on this earth just live without loving something or someone that's destiny. We can try steering destiny but it never fully goes in our directions that we really hope to steer it. Its being awhile since Rollin Taur visits his hometown, his dressing increase the village temperature; he was dress in mostly black with a small amount of red display from his undershirt conceal a red string around his neck. His felt hat was black with a red cloth tie around the hat; it matches his trench coat black with lines of red colour. The village appear to be in shades in the day, dark clouds floating in the sky and the large amount of vultures circling contribute to decrease in sunshine. He takes out his phone and call, when the person answers he analyze for a bit and realize the car honking on the next person phone was over a restaurant across the road. He continues talking to the female on the phone, after he walk over to the restaurant. He walks past a few tables, next he approaches the brightest smile that make him happy. It was Doctor Zioness Salvation his classmate and ex girlfriend. She studies demonology witchcraft and ancient Egyptian hieroglyphics she was also a member of Special Demon Academy. "The hunter you did not disappoint me; I was watching you a bit before I come out there" she smiles he interrupt her. "Why a wonderful Goddess hunt demon?" "Being marvelous is already a hard task, let SDA hunt the ugly demons since they have matching appearance; by the way were you watching me or admiring me" he starts laughing. "You never change Rollin Taur still the same person from high school days always acting childish, I of to admit you never fail to make me smile" she smiles again which brighten the pathway for Rollin Taur future. "No more test Doctor Salvation, congrats on banishing the coffin with the six john crows on it I read about it in the paper" he looks around the room wondering if anyone was listening. "Its being really long Zioness Salvation, I of to even congratulate for your PHD in Demonology and ancient Egyptian hieroglyphics." "Congrats again school did not turn you to fool, a colleague of mine study too hard, we hear stumbling in kitchen...." he looks around again. "He eat our pet dog, he claims the dog is Satan eye to this world and sacrifice of to make so he will take the poison" he hears some information that interest him so he pause his conversation for the moment. "Yeah boss, its a crazy story he was on them pills, he claims a blazing red eye beast with chains eat the molasses." The well dress gentleman only reply with yeah before start talking again. "He was burn as well boss badly, this morning at the hospital he tells me the bull start setting the place on fire and he hide and manage to escape." "I will handle it" he gives an assuring answer and leave without finishing his meal. Rollin Taur and Doctor Zioness Salvation decide to check old man George the senille elder to try and obtain information. They get directions from a little girl, the way to old man George home was off the village road, it was a small cave on a hillside and it only have entrance no exit. They climb over a few rocks before reaching the entrance. They approach a little wooden gate with damage paint up dolls head on both side. A black flag was flowing on the housetop with an inverse pentagram and a regular pentagram same colour close by. Symbols in various colours was all over the flags. There were writings in words on the flag it flow in the wind and make a howling sound. They approach the door the door knob has a horseshoe above it, there was a small circle on the door. The circle has an X through it one line longer than the other, it could signify we all do evil at times no one is perfect at anything. Rollin Taur almost call Senile George but he hesitates this almost happen because people hardly call him by just George senile before his name sound more intriguing to village folks. He is well known in town for his horrific crazy stories, most people see him as a crazy old man. Mr George!! Mr George!! Rollin Taur stop after two calls and listen after that he hear a shuffle in the house and call two more times. George step forward and open the door, "welcome to my sanctuary Special Demon

Academy I smell the purify metal that create your righteous pentagram from a few metres away." "I have been expecting you, I hear recruiting taking place every 6 year." He switches the topic "tell your lady friend behind the tree that a lizard is close to her hands" Senile George look at the tree. Doctor Salvation scream out and run from behind the tree brushing her clothes, she did not like lizards as she has an idea that George say behind tree and lizards she moves away before checking. "How did you see that??" Rollin Taur ask a man of his caliber know about superstition he meet a demon possess girl already and she know things from his past that he bury deep in his mind. What surprise Rollin Taur is that the people of the village abandon the stories this wise powerful man tell. "Why don't people believe the things you say?" Rollin Taur look at George. "My son even God people doubt I am the one with faith still trying to guide them" he look at Doctor Salvation while talking. "No need to be ashame my special friend, do all the good you can on earth now." "The devil is waiting on you to do evil you are a pure soul." "Talking of fear the Rolling Calf is afraid of dogs, even a beast like that have fear its just a part of nature" George check his mind trying to remember his fear his senile brain did not allow him to remember. "Cynophobia"Rollin Taur say the word and get back to listening to the old man. "There are things about this Rollin Taur that I don't want you to know its your destiny, Doctor Zioness Salvation you and Rollin Taur path design from your parents even decide to get kids." Senile George choose his words carefully he did not want Rollin Taur to know yet he might try to abandon his destiny and things get worst. "The Rolling Calf only have true strength to kill for revenge and who stand in the way of the beast innocent people have a chance against its evil it scares them to kill themselves" he tries his best to emphasize the words let them hear the Roaring Calf kills who stand in its way. "The killings are personal family curse the foul demon is wiping out the family tree, David at the bar father was the village enforcer leader, the same way he was evil and limp was pass down to his son." "Evil just choose this generation to attack, only four persons remain from the curse family tree Hades King who is fighting his own battles far away, Okill and snow." "You know the next person Taur find them if you hope to attempt and defeat the bull; here is a book hope the information can help you my fiery friend" George give a smile of hope. Rollin Taur mind was still trying to figure out what might be his destiny. "The Rolling Calf live under a big cotton tree Taur there is a map in the book, here is a tarred whip and a knife only your left hand can hurt the evil." "We are what they call curse sons of Adams Rollin Taur we are stubborn, now you must leave at once" his mood change. Doctor Zioness Salvation start walking before Rolling Taur after they walk away from the house Senile George shout his name "Taur doing the devil deeds does not make you his slave, you are not a demon you call my name four times the devil slave cannot do that" he smiles. He holds his hands far from his face next quickly remove the cloth tie around his head Rollin Taur see a third eye rotating in his forehead. After that the door make a hard slam and the horseshoe start making clanking sound continuously. Rollin Taur act calm and walk away wondering how he did not feel the evil presence. They drive toward the big cotton tree the option they have now is to repel the Rolling Calf from murdering its next victim before trying to defeat the Roaring Calf.

Meanwhile at jail: "Hey Officer can I get some molasses that's the only thing I need" Okill start shouting his words see if it would make a difference. "Ok your Highness its on the way sorry for the delay" he talks in a humble servant voice. He happens to have a bottle of molasses he walks over to Okill and open the bottle. "Open your hands" he sounds friendly. Okill obey the officer he spits in Okill hands he manage to escape some of the dirty saliva, Okill flash his hands rapidly, almost damaging himself on the iron bars. He tries to avoid any contact with the dirty cop spits. Okill start displaying rage on a next level punching the walls within the cell. "I will see you someday cop you dirty like your saliva" Okill stare at the cop with death in his eyes. "If it was up to me I chop off your hands murderer and beat you with them just for fun" he looks at Okill terrible. "Am no murderer am innocent when I get out of here....am going to..." he makes angry grimace. "Say it murderer" the police shout. "Ffffff...your wife" he starts trying to tease the cop he was attempting to use it as a procedure to ease his own troubles. "I Forgive your wife for passing a real man to marry a POL- Ice because you cold I know about the little girl" .... Okill start looking in the officer's eyes. "What little girl" he replies quickly. "Know what am finishing talking to you maybe later" he walks away speedily and the bottle of molasses drop on the ground and scatter all over the dirty floor. Out of nowhere a brindle cat appears and start drinking molasses. The police was about to get angry but he decides that might only make Okill see his angry mood. "Where did you come from?" "Better you get my molasses from the dirty ground than a murderer" he starts smiling after he take up the cat and realize it was friendly. "Come on furry friend don't drink from the ground am going to give you from a little kitty bowl" he walks away with the cat playing with it. Okill just stare like he was just alone at home watching TV and boredom take over.

Doctor Salvation approach the big cotton tree; she could feel a different temperature in the surrounding. There was a strong presence of evil that could let her faint if she doesn't stay strong. Rollin Taur look at her and notice she was looking pale. "Hey are you ok?" he walks closer to her. "Yeah just give me a small fifteen minutes break" she sounds angry. Rollin Taur assist her in finding a comfortable spot to sit. First Rollin Taur start chopping some trees of various size, he makes an inverse pentagram around the big cotton tree shape out with sticks. He sharpens some sticks and ram five deep in the ground around the inverse pentagram. The sharpen sticks were place in pairs apart and chains were use to connect the pair of sticks, the single one was attach with chains to the closest pair of pegs. Doctor Salvation feel better after she hear rustling in the bushes and think it was a lizard she run over to Rollin Taur working location. "Hades King you stink of death, did you come here to give the Rolling Calf drill instructions" Rollin Taur find sarcasm even in desperate dangerous times. "Adrienna my daughter was kill I move to my home from I get that news" Hades rest his shotgun on his shoulder. "You can take the warrior out the battle but you cannot take the battle out the warrior" he looks Rollin Taur in the eyes. Hades King is not just a warrior but a family man who interest is the well being of his family. He is a man who will walk on hot coals barefoot to protect his family. Doctor Salvation just keep staring at the warrior, she hears alot about his glory on the battlefield. "Ok warrior give me some warrior help I really need it" he says it in a sarcastic way. He keeps reading the book he receives from George the senile old man; the handwriting was difficult to read. "Guess you know what we going up against??? "Rollin Taur hand him the book. "No idea and i don't want to know I hear few rumours around town about some fiery eye beast" he grips his shotgun while talking. "I will kill anything that harm my family even if it's Okill, I visit the crazy old man he let me know where you were and give me a bit of details" he looks around at Rollin Taur work. "I have seen crazy things man doing evil deeds for pleasure only the horn is missing from their appearance" he talks while looking straight ahead as if he was visualizing memories. He hesitates for awhile next start talking "just know if Okill is responsible for my daughter death am going to kill him, am just helping you to stay away from the public" Rollin Taur stare at him and nod not to agreement for his mission or refreshing honest but to knowing what to expect. Rollin Taur think for awhile before talking "uuuum I think I learn it in a movie, slow is smooth, smoke is fast, forget it be careful warrior this is not just a physical battle." "You know I hear a story a farmer have a bull he loves so much, one day he was bringing it to the market to sell." "He spots other meat on display cover his bull eyes and say don't worry darling that only happen to animals who do bad things." After sharing that joke Hades King did not laugh he just nod his head and start taking instructions from Rolling Taur.

"Watch, absorb and understand warrior" Rollin Taur talk his words slow and clear. Rolling and Hades King cut trees to make a second inverse pentagram around the big cotton tree with King Hades assistance. They create two-point projecting upwards, this symbol of evil attracts sinister force overturn the proper order of the universe. Hades King start following Taur instructions to make a third one and use chains to connect the sharpen pegs. After they finish some of the tasks they go in the village to get some more supplies. After two inverse pentagrams with pairs of sharpen sticks bind by chains. Doctor Salvation draws a smaller pentagram with a circle inside with a bull head skeleton on the upside down flaming star. The circle was paint in red the inverse pentagram in white. She asks for assistance to draw a huge circle around the two other pentagrams. They stop Hades King at some point he wants to close the first and second circle but only the last one must be a complete circle the circle around the larger pentagram. After they finish Rollin Taur and Doctor Salvation recheck the circles next Doctor Salvation starts painting hieroglyphs on the point of the middle of the smallest pentagram. She looks around and start talking "I need organs from a live animal that you must bring here to slaughter in the circle Rollin Taur you know the procedures." "Warrior let's go hunt we need a live animal for this ritual" Taur signal Hades King and walk away. They leave Doctor Salvation to work on her tasks, approximately an hour later they return with a ram goat, that look injure. "Okay spill the blood in the circle and let the rest bleed out in that container" she points to a clay container with demonic carvings on it. Rollin Taur obey after that she place five burning red candles in five containers with the goat blood each candle was place on the largest pentagram. "Cut out the organs that match with the five sense they are vital for this ritual" she command King Hades

"Ok now let's seal back the last circle" she starts painting right away while talking. "Listen to me carefully once the evil is approaching all five candles will blow out in the wind" she talks in a loud concern tone. "You both are victims that's why I let you walk in the two circles, this will deceive the demon you are close and we make a move the last circle traps it and defeat the vicious demons." "Really now we are so proud of you Doctor Salvation" Rollin Taur look at her with straight face while talking. Hades King look at her and grip his shotgun tighter. "Hell arrest, shine heaven now, God with us" she finishes her chant in a strange language these erase thoughts of Rollin Taur and Hades King previous concerns. Night begin to fall and darkness follow in the night footsteps which lead to terror. Hades King agrees to watch first while Doctor Zioness Salvation and Rollin Taur take a sleep. On the hillside was quiet and night insects play their little music. The mosquitoes did not welcome their visitors with joy, they act like leech in a blood sucking competition against hunger. The dark night get darker with the intention of bringing rage and sorrow. Hades King hear a sound in the circle he looks and see a brindle cat that look lonely Doctor Salvation and Rollin ignore the mosquitoes and start their nap. He starts walking toward the circle to have a closer look, the brindle cat takes the dark side of tree. Hades King wake the two sleepers and point toward the big cotton tree. The blood in the cups start boiling when the heat of hell approach, the candles blow out. In the dark all three persons notice the humoungous blazing eyes in the dark at their feet level, it sizes and the blazing eyes reach the height of a grown man. The

Rolling Calf gallops with chains clanking and destroying the pentagram in its path until it reaches the circle. The fiery eye beast soon realize it's trap and the footsteps from the victims make it difficult to return to home instantly. The calf like creature whole body start blazing and the demons throw fire balls all over the circles. Hades King just stand there in disbelief and stare at death itself he never face anything like the Rolling Calf on the battlefield. He shivers in fear when the clanking terrifying chains drag this cause Hades King whole body to paralyze he drop his shotgun on the ground he looks in the demon eyes. Hades King conquer his fear and shoot once at the fiery beast it seems to have no effect. He shoots again and the Roaring calf timing the bullet as it tries to break the barrier of the third circle, a ball of fire release from its tail and connect with the bullet. The bullet did not past the third circle it reaches the destination which was on the line of the portal and the real world. The Rolling Calf expectation occur its action cause a tiny explosion. The Roaring calf realize an open and rush but the portal was closing, the demon intelligence tells it that it cannot go through, it sends a fireball from its tail at a rapid speed. The portal close and the Rolling Calf start howling loud the area within the circle start shaking like an earthquake. Doctor Salvation just stand and observe she know that she has to figure a way to save their lives and wild actions will not help. For safety Rolling Taur decide to perform a ritual he learn from the book he dig a hole and bury a cotton ball in it, then pour rum over the area and start a fire. He was rushing to perform the ritual the top of the container with the rum cut his hand, the top cover by the cork break and leave sharp edges that Taur did notice in the dark. Rollin Taur blood mix with the rum it get contaminate. The Rollin Calf do some damage with the fireballs but no one notice, one of the fire ball manage to set a root of bamboos on fire. The bamboos start

exploding and the fire blaze because the root contains dry bamboos. The

bamboos start dropping, the first close to the third circle, the second was

shorter than the first. The third one drop right in the third circle,

the thud of the bamboos informs the Rolling Calf that freedom was close.

It takes actions rapidly it was hungry for freedom the fiery creature rush

to get a belly full of freedom. The beast gallops to the end of the third

circle in line with the bamboo and rail a few times until it exit the third

circle. Rollin Taur draw for his tarred whip and move toward the Roaring

Calf the beast use it clanking chains and pull up chain with pegs on both

end. The Rolling Calf use its clanking chains and draw up a pair of pegs

and fling it toward Rollin Taur, he hears the swooshing and clanking

sounds his reflex let him dive to one side he drops hard on the ground. He

lies for a few seconds to ease the pain that infiltrate his body. He loses the

whip Hades King take up the whip in his right hand. The demons start

roaring and rolling toward Hades and Doctor Salvation. Swiiiish!! Hades

King slap at the Rolling Calf the beast was going to get strike on its not

side. The beast goes on its front feet and hoist the back feet in the air, the

whip barely miss its side. He makes a few more attempts but it was in vain

it bounce off the beast. The Roaring Calf was intelligent it notices either

the whip or the user was not effective. It pretends like it was scare of

Hades King and run away for a bit, Rollin Taur see the actions but he could

not give Hades the instructions to use the whip the roaring demon was an

intelligent disaster from hell. The Rolling Calf start galloping it charge past

and its clanking chains get fiery and wrap around Hades King feet and

drag him it pick him like a angry parents dragging a stubborn kid hand. He

lose the tarred whip and the rightful owner reclaim it. The brave man shout for help while being drag part of his pants was ablaze on fire.

"Satanam aliosque spiritus malignos, vade retro satana" Doctor Salvation

chant this get the Rolling Calf attention she was a big threat; it gallops fast

toward Doctor Salvation galloping with rage. It drags Hades King for a

while before letting off the baggage in a trench. The fiery beast charge at

full speed Rollin Taur step in front of Doctor Salvation he wait until the

demon was close he switch the tarred whip to his left hand. Swiiish!! The

whip crack it reach the Rolling Calf fiery skin it stumble for a bit and start

howling, a deep wound was on it side that bleed lava looking liquid. The

Rolling Calf rage turn madness its entire body was in fire it chains start

clanking hard and it throw random fireballs from its tail from a distance. A

next rumbling was in the circle memo reach hell that the gate is open, six

dark figures limping walk with chains around their boney neck and they

drag a coffin half open. The coffin glitter in various colours in the dark.

Doctor Salvation realize and move toward the circle one of the figure has

it hand through the complete circle that Doctor Salvation was trying to

seal. The skeleton figure h grab Dr Salvation hand it starts burning her,

before she start chanting. Swoooosh!! The hand drop on the ground from

Rollin Taur tarred whip the hand turns to maggots and centipedes which

return to the earth. He uses the whip to destroy the bamboos, each strike

send chunks of dirt flying everywhere Taur was trying to destroy the

pathway from hell to the real world. The Rolling Calf regain its focus on

destruction it charges toward the circle trying to get to what it see as

home hell, it realize the portal was still open.

Rolling Taur feel a burning bearable pain when he uses the whip, he ignores the pain. The Rolling Calf charge toward the circle like it hear a dinner bell and it was a convict just return from prison. Rollin Taur grip the tarred whip to make an attack, it catches on fire he of to drop it, the handle burns the area it falls on. The Rolling Calf hold a brake on its way to the circle. The moon had start shining, the howling of dogs was close by three big black dogs come out of the bush and attack the Rolling Calf. It howls and gallop in the shades from the moonshine, setting everything on fire in its path. Old man George appear he has three eyes he already checks out their well being he know they will manage. "This place is curse the demons that grab Doctor Salvation hand were slaves their master let them bury treasure next kill them and bury them with the treasure" Doctor Salvation sound frighten. Senile George hold her hand and observe it. He rubs an ointment with a lime and other spices smell "just minion demons soldier trying to upgrade in Satan Army" he holds down his head for a bit he uses to serve Satan at one point in his life now he might be a lone wolf who is masterless. "I feel their pain when the demons grab me the whipping from masters on the back, they were buried alive veins slit so they suffer in the grave" she sounds fearful. "Lets destroy this circle and get out of here, Doctor Salvation we will chant the rituals together" he walks closer to the circle. Rollin Taur did not trust him he analyze every words that escape old man George mouth. The circle was destroy and they walk away without looking back this curse place was not far from hell. The devil might visit someday; fire continue burning on earth the devil only need to add more fuel. Fire burn the area and the moonshine look down not bother by the fire.

<u>Tides of Flames Who Will Row the Boat to Hell????</u>

Meanwhile at Jail: Okill smell the musty smell in the jail cell it was no bother, his sorrowful thoughts was still on Adrienna. It pain him because he could not hurt a person he cares about so much about, he wonders if it was true that prison is curse and turn you into a friend killing psycho. His head start to hurt adapting to prison was easy for him but adapting for a crime he did not commit. "Why why W-H-Y" he says the word next he says it in a low tone after that his mouth move but no words. Toxic breath escape from his nostril it let him faint his world become darkness.

Knock!! Knock!! Knock!! Snow thinks few seconds before he acts, his life was different in the Caribbean he put hit on a federal agent and come home. He has a small door at the back of the house that he shows to his 11-year-old daughter Cadence. She gets instructions to stay away when he have a visitor he will call her when its someone she must see. "Daddy did i hear knocking it must be my best friend I miss talking to her" she gives him a lonely look while talking. "Go upstairs" he gives her a grave look she was the only thing in the world he was passionate about but she knows not to disobey him. After a 30 seconds he hear a hoarse tone call his name three times, he takes the secret door his protection was already on him. He dodges and watch the person that was calling him he goes closer and realize it was his crime partner. He still takes precautions and disguise his gun. It was a non civilize way to act even for a gangster but if anyone love his life and plan to live longer prefer to shoot and regret after. He opens the door his partner start smiling his silver teeth look like fang in the dark. "Wassup blood, when am I getting mine my weight is light" Snow talk and draw up his pants waist to give his crime partner clue. "I am working on it Snow it take times this is not Miami; I hear babies have AK in their stroller" the man start laughing. "Maaan you still cold boy can't you invite an old crime partner in your house, we use to make them bleed" he starts talking furiously while rotating his head. Snow walk away leave him standing he did not say a next word to the man. The man start walking away Snow open the door "yow don't ever use the way you see life to believe I see it the same way, I mean you can even take the house you save my life" Snow nod his head in respect to the man. "Now that's Snow you have me thinking that Miami get you all Mafia don't wanna flick with the local killer; I kill for cheap am proud of it, that's were you start as well Snow" he looks around after finishing his statement. "Your errand boy from back in the days Okill is in jail, I hear he kill them gang members terrible think you might not want to see him in hell." "If I know that he has the killer ambition I would have recommend him to you, on the other hand maybe you would not be having this conversation or the boy go with crime further." "That si-sicko no psycho I think.... I mean they rape his mother and slash her throat, she is the last parent and remaining family that he cares about." Snow crime partner release his gangster chronicle to the bird of the same feather that he flocks with.

Snow nod is head "he is a good kid a lot of principles to have just a mother, always on time not trouble maker like us" Snow talk in a respectful way. "You know once I stop that kid from setting a church on fire?" Snow talk and look directly in his partner in crime eyes. "A kid steals his ice cream that he was to bring home for his mom, long story short I see him with the match and gas." "The lady that beat him because he fights the other kid was in the church with the kid that steal the ice cream." "They were both in a small board church, the kid could not wait for revenge he decides to burn the church" Snow talk with excitement like he see a protégé. "Cannot help him now I only care about one thing now" he draws his hand across his face and make a sigh after he finish talking. "Where is Cadence???" "Hope you dont trust that crackhead mom, I hear in the street she involves in human trafficking for a crime boss" his partner in crime sound concern. "She is not around she is ok where she at, crackhead mom, i would not want to meet the father" Snow talk in a coarse low angry voice. His partner in crime rapidly switch the nature of his conversation. "You remember that OG you kill before going Miami?" he looks at Snow he seems clueless. "No I dont remember my local crime" Snow give a sly smile. "The one that you kill because he threatens you that he will rape and kill your little daughter in front of you" he looks in Snow eyes and there was none verbal communication Snow mood change. "Cadence is not here, just like that OG I guess, the thing is though Cadence is at her Aunt that OG might be in gangsters Paradise." He lies about his daughter he still did not trust his crime partner. "His son hear you kill the OG and put a contract on your head so I hear did you kill his father for real???" "You never mention that" he talks while texting on his phone. Snow grab after the phone and miss the device he takes out his gun "so you a snitch now, who are you working for??" "Let me check your phone" he looks at his partner in crime he hesitates to give Snow the phone. He has a wild suspicious fearful look on his face. Snow start laughing "you almost brave but I see the fear in your eyes I kill and mince up that OG; bury him under the big cotton tree." Snow make movements with his hands. His partner in crime put his phone on a table, its start ringing he look at the phone it was an unknown caller. "Answer it Snow you might hear who am working for" he starts laughing loudly. Snow laugh and answer the phone and put it on speaker "kill Snow...the man on the phone sound vex and impatient. Click!! Click!! Snow have a gun pointing at him. "Am sorry maaaan you just got it coming, my wife is sick, three teenagers daughter pregnant; I hear on the streets you in Miami buying Lambo, just for pet dogs you see loyal to you" he sound like tears was close to run from his eyes. "Even my mongrel dog is loyal he just wants bones, I collect money from four different persons to kill you" he talk and push the gun back and forth. "Too much enemies Snow you are too cold you the type to let me die poor" he hiss his teeth after he finish talking. "Look on the bright side you are the last person am going to kill; I see you kill your cousin Snow I dont kill you already because you are like an unstable kid" he nod a few times testifying to his words. "You keep a party years ago I wait five hours in the dark I hear you went to church with an old lady you promise her, you sleep at church that night you too good Snow" he starts laughing as he was delightful he achieve something. "How did you fall in Jamaica Snow??" God daaaammnn!! His partner in crime have the situation under control he was having fun. Snow laugh loudly "my dog is loyal than you dawg." His crime partner from the past start getting nervous" you still going to die poor, look at the bright side am going to take care of your family, I hear you abuse those girls; I might give your wife some loving." "She might call me God or Oooh God since I get rid of her problems." "Yow dawg don't let this rat blood splash on me; I fear leptospirosis drive the car and bury him under the big cotton tree" Snow start sounding cruel in his tone. "Yes Master Snow with pleasure" a humble servant like voice come from the dark side of the room.

Knock!! Knock!! Knock!! A few seconds past before they could think of opening the door it was on fire when it blasts off and the Rolling Calf look inside. Only Snow get the option to look death in the eyes, he was shock and the Rolling Calf look at him and gallop across the door. Snow partner in crime get a few escape options he drops and shoot in the corner the voice in the corner stumble in the dark. There was clanking of chains outside, the Rolling Calf stay at the doorway and throw fire balls that set the house on fire. Snow hear a shot and his foot become numb, his crime partner was shooting. Snow return shots while his injure foot drag on the ground. He was moving toward Cadence, the room he send Cadence was already blazing on fire. The Rolling Calf stand outside and howl loudly, a piece of board drops on Snow friend and sink him under the board floor. With fear Snow move toward the door way, the Roaring Calf fiery eyes was blazing and charge toward Snow....

"We cannot make it to two location Rollin Taur, Dr Salvation go to the jail, I will find Cadence she survives it seems Snow fall, Rollin Taur you know as well know why not share the information?" Senile George look at

Rollin Taur in a strange way. "You senile as usual but that's the best idea, Rollin Taur feel strange from the ritual he feels the pain of souls the Rolling Calf consume. Hades King drive the vehicle close to Snow home "I am going to need a stop soon up by the old church, the little girl is all alone in the dark running take care especially Dr Salvation" Senile George voice express his concerns for the poor innocent souls. "We close to the church old man be specific where you want to stop, we don't have enough time I got someone to ki...". Hades King statement was disturbing by the flapping of bird wings. He stops and look around Senile George was outside the vehicle and in the dark his movements toward his location make his body look like a cloud floating. "Crazy old man this is not a horse don't jump out moving vehicle" Hades shout at him his rage blind him to the events that take place quick time. Rollin Taur and Doctor Salvation was aware but as demon Slayers they observe the situation because it's life and death. Hades King speed toward the direction of the jail where hell itself was waiting.

Meanwhile at the jail: The brindle cat walks up to Okill and lick off his face, this did not wake him he just lies similar to playing possum. The brindle cat walks in the darker part of the jail untill it disappears out of sight. A police officer walks while checking the jail cells, he has a habit roll up pieces of paper and throw them everywhere. "There go janitor work to do, you tell the boss about my street hustle I do everything to make your life a living hell" he talks in an evil voice. He throws the piece of paper in the air it did not drop, he shines the flash light he sees the paper suspend in the air. He shines light and walk all the other pieces of paper were suspend in the air floating and his eyes did not allow him to see what suspend the pieces of paper. He shines his light again and see web with fly and a piece of paper in the web. After a few seconds the pieces of paper fall to the ground. His curiosity almost let him trip over a goat rope he was about to curse. He hears the bleating of a goat in the dark and use his light to follow the rope, he notices a black and white goat with spots. "What the hell is this?" he was surprise the goat was in a jail cell and the rope attach to a next cell. He pulls the rope from where it was tie and pull the next jail cell, the goat head was in a corner. He drags the rope and he end up on his buttocks he starts making sliding movements to get up, the rope turns to fire and the goat turn around there was no head. He crawls on his two hand first until he stands and start running, there was a loud noise and the cell door start melting like lava. He run displaying dyspnea he drop on the ground, he move on hands and feet on the ground like an animal he push a door and head down the stairway. The rumbling down the stairway was fear from the cop it even let him trip over even with no obstacles in the way. The loud clanking of chains get the police attention they move toward the location of Okill jail cell. The superintendent leads the way they step cautiously when they approach Okill location, one officer advance by command from the superintendent. He moves unwilling he find Okill cell and shine his light he was there on the floor, "supe he need help he is knockout on the floor" he stutter over a few words. Before the supe could answer the sound from clanking chains start moving toward them, the roaring calf was fully ablaze it howl. When the supe see the terror with the large ball of fire "Fire!!" he shouts it out loud. The bullets display no effect on the roaring calf it moves in different directions releasing toxic smoke and at the same tricking the officers that the bullets were effective; the bull howl loud and act as if it was dodging the shots. The nine officers and the superintendent drop their guns and start moving in various directions.

Hades King drive to the entrance of the police station this vehicle match his description it could be brutal and brave. Rollin Taur was sitting in the front seat he feeling a burning inside his body, he was about to talk fire come out his mouth. His nostrils release toxic smoke it causes Hades and Doctor Salvation to faint and the vehicle connect in the wall of the station. Hades King and Doctor Salvation were unconscious but not injure badly, Rollin Taur notice his changes he realizes they were not injure badly, he accepts his changes and know he will of to try and defeat the Roaring Calf alone. Hades King and Doctor Salvation gain conciousness after a few minutes. Rollin Taur start predicting the bull movements it aims was to burn and weaken the first floor with fire and let it collapse. One of the police man take up his gun he was a weaker evil soul the Roaring Calf have him under a demonic spell. "Mom" he calls. He was in a trance he visions his little brother climbing a tall tree to get a bird nest he call and start bawling. His brother was in the tree top the birds furiously attack him he slips and drop on his head it stuck in the ground. It makes a cracking sound again his head in the ground and his body falling over till his body drop flat. The police man hears a laughing, he look around a next man was pointing laughing and celebrating he find a gun and point it on the man. His partner was shock all the other guns was behind this officer the other gain their consciousness. In his dream like state he points the gun everywhere, staring wildly at the policemen. His partners try to avoid the gun it was a shotgun and they were close. They bend down stumble and fall over each other. He just come back to his sense and ask what happen everyone look at him weird. "Everyone doing ok?" the superintendent ask. "Only feel tiresome and draining and my head hurt and feel like my head on fire, just have a dream the convict I shoot and kill five years ago was raping my 1-year-old daughter" one of the officer talk with a relief voice. "Let's get out of here I hear sound like fire blazing the convict seems to escape in this disaster I don't see him" the superintendent command was of interest even the weak develop strength they make fast movements to meet fire at the finish line.

    The Rolling Calf know Doctor Salvation was a threat and she was close by the Rolling Calf power and intelligence decline and the toxic smoke clear away slowly. It starts rolling toward the second floor tearing down the stronger wall and set the strong walls on fire. The Rolling Calf loud clanking chains echo in the building; Rollin Taur have his tarred whip in his hand he waits in the walkway around the corner leading to the stairway. The Roaring Calf did not take that way it tears a new hole in the wall like a weather it predicts Rollin Taur movements like their mind was attach. The Roaring Calf create a flame prison for Rollin Taur he could not escape easily the circle of fire around him was way up to the ceiling. The Rolling Calf gallop toward the the first floor, it clanking chains on the stairway echo. Dr Salvation hear the horrifying noise and prepares for the danger. The Rolling Calf head show first and it take a few seconds before it shows it entire fiery body. Dr Salvation and the Rolling Calf make eye to eye contact it give a dark look and set ablaze on fire toward her, Hades

King come out and start shooting his shotgun a piece of the bull horn tear get damage. A large wound was it its side that bleed lava. The bullets get sprinkle with holy water earlier, the Roaring Calf know it was lethal it rages and howl and start throwing fire balls from its tail while taking cover. The loud terrifying clanking chains decrease it barely draw. The Rolling Calf push out its head and draw back fast Hades King fire his ammo was getting low the Roaring Calf tactics work. The Roaring Calf learn some militancy from Hades King and use it against him. The Roaring Calf notice a fan in the ceiling it throws a ball of fire and the fan falls on Hades King the shotgun drops. The fiery demon charges and Doctor Salvation chant "vade retro satana holy holy holy in the name of Michael and the archangels I condemn you to hell." The Roaring Calf slow down and charge outside and start setting fire around the entire building.

Okill wake up in a dark room that look like an office he was sleeping but he feels like someone was dragging him and he hear loud clanking chains. He hears sound of fire blazing outside he pull the door and run down the stairway Okill cross path with Doctor Salvation. "What's happening here??" Okill ask Dr Salvation questions as if she owe him an explanation. There was no time to answer they hear chains clanking coming down the stairway, Doctor Salvation hear snorting and smells smoke "cover your nose quickly" she wastes little time in getting the message across deliver because she of to secure her safety. "Hey Officers thank God, first am so happy to see police I of to talk the truth" Okill sound delightful. The officers turn round and start firing after Okill he dodge. "Stop!! Stop!! Doctor Salvation shout. They still fire "go to hell horn beast" one of the officer crying while shooting. The Roaring Calf was knowledgeable it cannot take revenge against the sinners but it can find way to make them hurt themselves. It charges fast through other sections of the first floor while the fire blaze around the station. Doctor Salvation walk and test the fire she realizes she did not feel any heat; it was a trick to keep them in the building. She finds a way to convince the officers; she put her hand in the fire the top of the building coming down help as well, one officer could not take the risk he has his newborn daughter to live for. He covers his head with his uniform and charge outside the others notice and follow Doctor Salvation advice she let the officers bring Hades King who was injure and unconscious the fan hit him hard his head was bleeding. The officers try to get her out as well they notice she was stubborn and the building was falling. They leave her they just could not understand the codes of a demon slayer. They escape from the fire and smoke they still look back to see how she was doing untill that option was no longer available to the officers. Okill was aware the danger of getting shot, was no longer a threat he advances toward the lower floor feeling pain he cannot explain and his skin feel like it was on fire he stumbles in the dark. Every second he moves his head swiftly and look around, he keep hearing clanking chains. He advances toward escaping out the burning building. He races toward the entrance at a fast pace and keep looking behind him as if he was getting chase by cops.

        Rollin Taur limp in the dark he looks at his left hand it was getting black and it smell like something was burning. He hears the sounds and look toward the lower floor, the demon start utilizing way to confuse and distract Doctor Salvation it gallops fast and use its chains to fling objects, it throws fireballs randomly. For a demon she faces before Doctor Salvation could feel the terror coming straight from hell. For safety she sprinkles a double circle of holy water around the area she stands. Rollin Taur keep predicting the Rolling Calf movements Doctor Salvation was a powerful threat the Devil would rejoice knowing he defeat one of God strong soldier. Rollin Taur chant in a strange language use a knife to cut himself, next stab the knife in the ground. It was the same knife with ancient symbols that he gets from Senille George earlier. He put the tarred whip in his left hand, it starts burning it make a sizzling sound and smoke rise he bawl in agonizing pain. His tarred whip and left hand blaze red hot hell fire that behave angry rising and falling fiercely. He attacks a part of the fire jail circle after a few attacks the barrier break there was an explosion Rollin Taur dive to the location his mind send him. The Rolling Calf charge outside fiercely with the objective of hoping Dr Salvation drop guard to try protect the people outside. She uses the time wisely she uses a pen like object fill with blood and draw an inverse pentagram it was not done close to perfection. The Roaring Calf change its actions and start galloping back and forth through the station let the structure get weaken. Okill pick up Hades King shot gun fill with holy water bullets and point it at Dr Salvation, there was two black bump on his forehead, he starts snorting loudly, smoke escape from his nostrils. He fires the gun there was a whip around his hand, his hand was drag down by Rollin Taur tarred whip, it wraps around his hand. Rollin Taur whip send his heavy body floating across the room. Rollin Taur only objective was to protect Doctor Salvation because he knows the Rolling Calf dark intentions, he attempt to predict its movements. The Rolling Calf mind set and soul was similar but their speed was different, his attempt only let fire sparks on the ground and debris with chunk of objects flying when he attacks with the tarred whip. Dr Salvation begin to chant "vades retro satana, go back satan." The beast still continues its perilous fiery journey. She continues chanting "go back to hell devil, fahr zur holle tuefel, vete al diablo diablo; aller au diable du-te in diavolul iadului." The chanting was affecting the Roaring Calf. It gallops past Rollin Taur and make a sharp stop and charge toward Doctor Salvation blazing with hell fire, she gets the shotgun and fire it tear off a small piece of the Rolling Calf face and slow it down. The Roaring Calf make a sharp stop when she sprinkles a bit of holy water this keep off the demon. Doctor Salvation drop to the floor the battle leaves her weak, blood flow through her nose she was on her knees. The Rolling Calf see its chance and charge toward her, the demon anxiety to kill her block its intelligence; the demonic creature human foot step in the inverse pentagram. That could hold the demons for awhile untill she can figure a way to defeat the demon she chants "thy soul is curse butcher I condemn thee to hell." A pool of boiling blood start to appear around the Roaring Calf it gets furious and howl loudly its terrifying chains clank loud. Swiiissh!! The tarred whip fire blaze fierce along with Rollin left hand the whip reaches the fiery beast body the wound almost seperate the beast in two halves, it howls in pain. It still tries to attack "Rollin....!!" Doctor Salvation shout to get his attention next throw a bottle fill with liquid in mid air. When it was in range with the demon, Rollin Taur swiftly switch the tarred whip to his left hand, the hunter hand and the whip turn hell fire. He slaps the bottle in mid air it breaks and send liquid all over the place, some of the splinters pierce the Rolling Calf skin, the liquid make contact with its body and make a sizzling sound. The Roaring Calf stumble and drop to the ground its snorting get low and fire barely escape its nostril. The beast still find strength to crawl a little distance from the circle it looks in Rollin Taur eye in a pitiful way he could feel the creatutre pain but a demon is a demon. He look in its eyes and feel the family bloodline curse, in the bull eyes he see into its soul and see the butcher with his face still melting off from the burning fire, he try to talk but no word come out his tongue was gone. He takes out his knife and plunge the Roaring Calf in the head a few times. A few claw grips the demon body and start drawing it back into the pool of boiling blood, the demonic creature disappear and the boiling blood start decrease in size.

A chain flies out the boiling blood and grip Rollin Taur foot; the contact produce a sizzling sound follow by Rollin Taur foot on fire. A few seconds after a dark black smoke release and Rollin Taur reality turn to a trance. He gets flash backs and see the Rolling Calf pain in his trance the flash backs feel like reality to Rollin Taur. His visions were blurry a few seconds after he start seeing a bit clearer. He hears a woman voice complaining he did not hear the full conversation in his sleep like state "Its your son filthy bloody butcher, I was drunk the night, am so ashame I put myself with you." "Now my good husband is going psycho I wish i could change this; you take advantage of me, I won't forgive you I swear on my life am going to let my witch grandma obeah you bloody butcher" she bawls and weep while talking. The butcher just keeps walking away humble she walks behind the butcher and curse. Rollin Taur see the husband sons work with the butcher he encourages his son to put stone under the butcher scales so his sins get heavier. Rollin Taur visions leave him heartbroken. In Rollin Taur mind the lady cursing the butcher get furious; the butcher tells the boy that he is the boy father. She denies the boy of the information and get furious claiming the butcher was a liar and animal bandit. "Son I was rape and the same butcher he is a wicked man; he is going to let you lose me he is not a good man" she curses the butcher in her conversation. After awhile Rollin Taur was in a wilderness he hears the cursing lady voice in his visions; out of nowhere her body just drop in front of him after that a group of demonic looking vultures start circling her body. Rollin Taur realize from an old photo the boy was his father and the other Psycho son was Okill father. Psycho appear in Rollin Taur vision he let the boy turn Judas against his father and tell lies that the butcher steal animals. Psycho appearance in Rollin Trance vision show Psycho smiling his canines have sharp points, he gives a wicked grin and his eyes was red like blood. His visions were still blurry he feel like he was in the cold and someone was pulling him closer to heat. "Vade retro Santana" Dr Zioness Salvation chant furiously this revive Rollin Taur a bit he already drops his demon hunter knife and tarred whip. He shiver like he was in a seizure, his eyes turn white and he was sweating heavily until sweat run and glisten. The pool of boiling blood already start expanding again he look down in the depths of hell and see souls trying to escape while they drag back each other. Doctor Salvation chant even louder and he come out the trance like state. The blood fade away and the dark deep hell hole that try to consume Rollin Taur close up. Rollin Taur was still sweating extra hard hell feel like it was boiling water on his skin for a few minutes. There was no sign of the inverse pentagram it disappears with the pool of boiling blood. The paramedics and firemen approach they take up Okill, the firemen were confuse there was no fire and they hear the station was on fire. They look around to analyse the damage of the prison ceilings and foundation only signs were ashes with few small damages on the structure. They scratch their heads attempting to see signs of great damage the demonic dark beast creates. Doctor Salvation walk for a few yards "Rol...." she drop on her face and blood run from close to her face it soak the dry dirt. Rollin Taur turn around and rush to her body and shout for help while crying. The paramedics put her on the stretcher her body was lifeless, her head slowly turn to Rollin Taur direction and her nose bleed continue there was a tiny ball of fire in her eyes. Why!! Whhhhyyy!! He bawls and beat the ground looking to the sky and asking "these are the consequences and sacrifices of our good battles." "I am the one that kill, she is just trying to protect the innocents" he shouts at the top his voice tears flowing in his mouth with spit this let his words decrease in clarity. The individuals around try to comfort Rollin Taur but it was in vain, he was not in the world at the moment the world was on his shoulder. He plans to sit there alone for the moment until the crowd slowly scatter due to police investigations. He walks on the lonely road in the middle for a while a vehicle was approaching. It stops and honk behind him next drive past him take a turn off. He continues walking in the middle of the road until he go down a hill and disappear out of sight. Conquering the Roaring Calf was like yesteday for Rollin Taur he have a heavy heart that will beat untill he reach the grave. The village folks feel a lighter atmosphere like they were enclose in a small room with crowd and the toxic smoke clear away. Some did not believe the stories but the death and terrors have them considering if there was any existence of the fiery eye beast the Rolling Calf. The cane season did not bring sweetness but horrific sorrow, the area that Doctor Zioness Salvation create the inverse pentagram reappear the pentagram glow bright red fire below the surface a three teeth fork stab the surface it barely crack. A police man was walking away from that area but he did not look back to notice the bright fire light emitting. Maybe it was for his own good that he misses the chance to see the ugly face of sorrow that dwell in the Rolling Calf home. The stories of the Rolling Calf live on and terror sparks from people tongue and they blaze on fire with fear when they hear about the Rolling Calf deeds in the once peaceful humble village.

REDEMPTION: Good to BE Bad And Bad To BE Good (06.06.16)

It was cane season in the village that develop over the years; the annual event starts in the village people dance around the spot of the cotton tree and drink liquor. The man in red and black with his head wrap with a turban wave his big flag five ladies dance and sing in circle. Under the gigantic cotton tree, there was a bull head in the way he crushes it and laugh and throw the bull head at the root of cotton tree. He enjoys the moment laughing and singing the night approach and lock off the party. Everyone walk home in a happy mood expecting to enjoy the next year.

Okill lie in a psychiatric home, he keeps shouting "we did not kill the kid, don't curse me for that, it's coming I hear the chains." In another room the 7 pm news start "drugs kingpin Anthony Fierce otherwise known as Snow wake out of his coma today he will be sentence at a later date...." Power cut the tv shut off and the place witness darkness. There was the sound of generators and electricity was active in the building. There was talking in the other room it was a female voice "girl I hear a butcher was trample to death by his bull that he uses to abuse physicallly." The lady voice continues talking "well anyone eat that beef might turn a Rolling Calf, if the butcher dont turn first and terrorize the streets" she starts laughing, the laughing fade away in the building.

Senile George look at the TV for awhile in silence" Cadence bring me the big black book" he commands. "Okay master I am going to get it" she speaks with a high level of respect. She returns with the book with large skull heads on the cover. He signals to Cadence to join him and they read and start laughing like they receive salvation from heaven.

"Daddy close your foot; remember you tell me to close mine" Rollin Taur daughter Zioness show attitude when she commands her father about principles. "Yeah thanks for reminding me my bundle of big lovable joy, where is your brother Cuceritor?" "He is outside using that stupid tarred whip of his to target bottles, the other kids say he is a wacko" she pushes her mouth up at him. "First am hearing that word don't sound good to me might let your teeth rot when you use that word" he talks and turn his head away to make a small chuckle. "I drink one bottle of molasses you know the rat that touch the other bottle" he talks in a voice pretending angry. She tries to cover her mouth to hide the evidence he run at her and hug her up acting childish "you little rat, you little little two feet rat." Swish!!! Rollin Taur turn around and see Cuceritor he holds down his head and his felt hat hide his face. "Howdy cowboy, put down the whip and get ready for bed" he endorses his mature father voice with a command to Cuceritor. "Hurry up cowboy I am going to tell you a story" he tries to motivate the kid to get his tasks done faster. "Not again dad, the same scary one that let me scare I hardly could sleep, I want to hear about princess riding dragon" Zioness sound scary. "The cowboy will protect you, plus the princess riding dragons at times you hardly can tell which is the princess or dragon" Rollin Taur talk in a mocking voice and laugh. Cuceritor return gasping a bit "you can start now dad please" he talks with excitement. "Am going for the book but am going to get something else its urgent he look at his phone, about thirty minutes" he walk off and shout the rest of his statement. The kids lie there in silence suddenly they hear the clanking of chains and three loud knocks on the door, there was a shadow at the door. Cuceritor walk toward the door and open it the big black dog jump on him, it manages to escape from it's kennel again taking the chain with it. Rollin Taur return he admire the kids before talking "I was testing your bravery; it was the dog I was checking on but Scythe here doing fine have fun with him before I return him kids." Scythe bark at Rollin Taur angrily for a while like he was a stranger next the dog gets friendly and start wagging its tail. Rollin Taur step back a bit from the dog with a bit of fear next he moves toward it when it get less threatening. "Someday day Cuceritor Invige Taur the book will be yours, share the information with your sister; its destiny you will understand someday son" he holds down his head and talk in a low sad voice but the kids did not notice. Rollin Taur close the book "all of us dont believe in books we say books or myth just know the idea just did not appear like that its from somewhere...." he changes the mood. "For tahta John a-dead, de oda nite one rollin-calf lick him eena him head, that's the poem am going to read" he struggles over the pronunciation of some of the words in Patois a local language. He read the poem the kids listen, "now someone tell me the name of the person who write that poem?" Rollin Taur hear no answer and look, the kids drop asleep. "Good night Zioness and Cuceri Invige Taur, cuceritor al taurului conqueror of demons, god nignt fiu si cuceritor al demonilor" he looks at them and walk toward the door. The light shine through the window, Rollin Taur back appear to be rigid flesh look like a rope wrap across him. He steps outside he look up in the sky from under his felt hat, notice there was no moonshine he drink a bottle of molasses and went back in the house.

     "Lady are you ready??" Hades King shout to Doctor Salvation. "Yeah I was born ready but this parent and demon slayer life is killing me" she sounds angry a bit. "The kids are good but now the Special Demon Academy and the church want me to hunt my own husband, they say a demon is going around killing criminals, am so confuse uuuggh!! "What a

Cow-incidence not a coincidence" she uses her expression of words with emotions. They continue the conversation while driving, on both end of the road there was blazing fire for a distance like hell was trying to part earth.

Two criminals attempt to rob an old lady for her purse, they get distract by the loud clanking sound of chains their hearings tell them the sound was distance away but it was approaching closer to them rapidly. Swish!!! A tarred whip on fire come through the door, the criminals were on the ground a sever hand blazing on fire was close to the criminal's body the old lady stand trembling in fear. Two pictures drop outside and start to burn the images on the picture did not have human appearance. The criminals body start bleeding all over hot red blood flow in the cracks and its seem to reach the darker depths, from deep down a loud voice howl sounding disapprove about events taking place on earth.

FINIS

<u>Jamaican Tale</u>: The Rolling Calf(adapted from the movie script/book The Fiery Eye Beast: Rolling Calf by Roland Brown)

Jamaican tale!! Jamaican tale!! The curse of the fiery eye beast the rolling calf, the demon slayer Rollin Taur, good versus evil bloody war, curse family forever scar. A time of mystical action, trouble actions strange reactions. Reality reveal a gruesome act, cannot save their souls from hell with sun block. Horrifying sound from the clanking chains, humongous blazing eye with the flames. It come at night in the country side, it fears dogs still you better hide. The tale lead us to believe it's superstitions, you get trick deception is evil missions. Zioness Salvation fight against the dark force, Rollin Taur tarred whip playing heavenly high notes. The Rolling Calf bring fear, grown man charging at barb wire skin no tear. The Rolling Calf bring death, Jamaican man almost drown in sweat, toxic smoke the Rolling Calf breath, trembling fear in everyone step. They trap the beast, intelligence never cease, even the undead cannot rest in peace. The devilish devil old wretch servant, eyes everywhere heaven-hell gift the death merchant.

Reality tradition and myth, amazing tale check out the script. Through determination of a humble Author, fiery tales escape the lips of the forefathers. Where there is a will there is a way, evil come and go protective Angels still stay. Reality still display fact, innocent blood spill no turning back. We hear from the old man, message to the young ones, tradition still on the land, go check it out on Amazon. How this tradition end, follow the link tell a friend, the next step your decision to see the end.

By: Roland Brown

<u>Frefre Grannie(Local Language:Patois)</u>

Oooiii!! Bwoy how fi yuh face suh wite an yuh pants suh tite, dat nuh rite inna yuh face blak an wite a fite maasah yuh kin mussi a fly weh lacka kite. Mi mumma mi fi seh vultra weh a nyam up wi cultra. Marcus mark us mo Marcus Gaaarvey, oonu a joke weh anuh Steve Harvey. Louise muss a grieve cultra a bruk dung lacka ol jeep, bare walking duppy weh naw sleep. Ebrybody affi duh as dem please lawd Gad wi Miss di gud ol Louise,

Bennett shi buil cultra neva bennie. Ooiiee!! Bwoy yuh face a pwile, nuh kayta suh nuh tell mi fi kibba mi mout dear chile, yuh fava gal muss gel yuh wah fi get style.

Ooiee!! Gal yuh nuh hab nuh pride, yuh fava side way crab weh back slide. Wah mek yuh bore yuh yiy top, yuh luk mash up lacka glass plate wen it drop. Yuh fava di puss weh litenin strike unda di pear tree, yuh ready fi baak mine mi ketch flea, pissie tail gal yuh betta flee. Oonu bun out oonu kin lacka di new time sinting weh dem call CD, tun up oonu music wen oonu si me. Dem deh poppy show tune cyah mek mi drop foot, oonu wile lacka cow mi back foot. Drop di song muss be a duppy or gunman, mek mi tek up mi foot inna mi han, likkle gal mine yuh pop yuh neck bout yuh a duh han stan wooooiee!!

Oiiee!! Bwoy an gal Kiss mi neck run dung tap mek, gwaan a KFC oonu su have fowl bret. Call mi mout amassi Liza missis Massa mi affi chat, di gud ol days muss bawn back. Doan blame mi seh mi ol, wen di sun touch mi dawk kin stil shine lacka gol. Galang dung a riba guh wash off, mussa set dem set oonu suh jus wah lef yaad. Ooiie!! Bwoy and gal oonu nuh healthy atall, bet if yuh get di hula hoop yuh stall, yuh waist aguh tan dung unda steady lacka wall. Ooiie!! Bwoy an gal oonu colour run weh mussi Maas Tom black puss, nuh friten fi oonu tek naw nuh logi prefa lib a back bush. Hehe!! Mi ole belly bottom bun mi wonda if a suh it soun, naw mek oonu tie up mi tongue. Caw mi affi chat wah mi si, anuh ebry butta puss si him fi lickie. A gwine try likkle English wi motto seh Out Of Many One People, outta many one people. Wi cultra a get run ova lacka vehicle, nuh gud bare evil. Wi culda tek it fi joke wen Mass Tata and Mass John a fite ova Ta Mary, nowadays how dem pale face people yah suh scary, betta wi guh back to shooting picheerie.

Massa mi dun chat oonu wi shoot mi back.....,gwaan guh luk a bus guh back a mi kuntry side, di sun a kum out oonu betta hide. just memba oonu pride yuh reap wah yuh sow, Fre Fre Grannie kno. Respect yuh self black or white doan be black tar and wah tun snow. Suh teck care mi dear chile stil lub oonu doan oonu fava kunumunu, just hol on pon oonu cultra nuh mek it miss oonu.

Roland S Brown

Cantankerous Granny(Adapt From FreFre Grannie)

Oiiiee boi!! Your style not my type your pants too tight, that's not right, smile and pain in your face emotional fight. Your joy take off like a flight, you use might to get stripes. Holy mother of Mary you are scary hair on the top none on the side, ooh so nowadays you trim even your pride, call you vulture, no dead meat here stop eating our culture. Marcus mark us more Marcus Gaaarvey, you act like a joke its not even funny like Steve Harvey. Louise Bennett will grieve our culture slow down like gramps old jeep, I only see walking zombie that don't sleep. Free world do as you please, everytime I think of heritage I miss Miss Louise, Bennett if culture was government she would be a Senate. Ooiiee!! Boi you act like a spoil child, you know you could be my child. I don't care dont tell me to close my mouth, I never tell you to close your facebook account. I don't understand, the way you dress or you a who man or woman? Better find a positive plan.

Ooiee!! Gal you lost your pride, in the dump your pride reside. Walking side way miss crab, let males passing you from hand to hand handouts handbags. Wonder why you pierce close to your eye brow Queen bee, I laugh at you hell raiser silly billy bee, below your knees is where your skirt should be. You remind me of the glass plate that get damaged, you claim you hot no you not hot hot porridge, that's cold all about the cash protect your soul, hold up your heads be bold. You look frighten are you cousin with my timid old cat that lightning strike under a pear tree, ready to bark at me, those nails you ready to claw at me. Giddy Gal you better flee, Lassie careful someone will contract flea, you just a baby yet no respect for the old lady, roll your eyes look at me well one of us is crazy. Our heritage burn similar to a CD, wish I could turn off this time like TV. Mumbo jumbos songs will not let me dance, play Ben E King i will definitely take a chance. Your dance wild like animal, keep the wildness at a minimal. Let me hear this song I was born by the river, cantankerous granny do dance moves even when they shiver, swing the old hip two times your eyes get addicted quicker, might do a drunken dance without the liquor. Watch your neck with your hand stand, you just trying to impress to let that boi stand, seeking attention find the grand stand, seek a better plan.

Oiiee!! Boi and gal laugh till my old belly hurt, look at that clown over there in a tight shirt, better not wear that to church, you deny freedom of movement don't know your worth. You just all about KFC, come to my home get GFC, granny famous cooking, everyone say its finger licking. Nobody does it better, mmhmmm granny cooking let tummy warm like sweater, KFC craze some of you light middle name should be bird feather. Again don't tell me to shut up the good old days must reborn, hope the featherweight can manage the storm. Blame me that am old my personality still glitter, oops bet you cannot find me on twitter, for your eyes only that's how you like my picture. You give love a bad name, I will listen Bon Jovi not ashamed, heritage dying all of us will of to take the blame. Ooiie!! Boi and gal your characteristics is like plastic easy to melt, you look stupid like when Tom the drunkard cannot find his felt, when its right on his head, hardly can look eyelids seems to be heavy heavy lead. Ooiie!! Boi and gal colour should never run away like scapegoat, your modern clothes lot of tears come to my farm i need a scare crow. Your technicalogy if that's how its pronounce, it will never stop my heritage from getting announce, everywhere in my blood if you check it by the ounce. Hehe!! My bunion burn on my heel, not terrible like the way modern people let me feel, i spit in fire when i have a cold am a old piece of steel. I talk what I see, blame the persons talking what they never do on

CD, I see four young individuals signal lost no 4 G, this world is like fairytale okie dokie. Add this to the commandants united we stand, divided we fall, do something don't block the way modern days wall, promote your heritage when your name is call. It was all a dream thanks Martin Luther, you pave the way for a brighter future.

Our culture is like a vehicle, its revving now more evil, minds too feeble there is no love in a needle. There was jokes when Bartholomew and John fighting over aunty Mary, nowadays modern demons really scary, in my days only a few birds will of to fear me. I am finishing talking don't want to get insulin shot, I know its not current alone let persons get shock. Peacefully returning to my countryside, the sun coming out nowadays vampire better hide,just remember your pride. You reap what you sow, cantankerous granny know, only you can let your heads bow, don't be the bow that shoot the arrow. Respect yourself black or white the zebra survive with the mixture, assist each other, motivation to see a bigger picture. So take care my dear children don't be nincompoops, prefer its a camera everytime you shoot. Hold on strong to your culture, don't search for the power you are the power like rain your blessings will shower.

Roland S Brown

<u>Workout</u>

Touching touching her most sensitive body parts, legs act like enemies the way they stay apart, slow fast slow describe a better start. My touch feel like ice cold icy water crawling down your spines, style blow your mind, destiny I will make you mine. Guess am a magician, clothes disappear before you see the wand, what's in my pants strong strong, will rise before I see a girl do her hand stand. Reverse the word no to on click click turning you on, adjust the volume before we collide our souls turning one. Next level kissing on your neck before you get to stretching with the sweat, you will win the race let's make a bet, better I have you bathe in sweat, than turn up short dyspnea short of breath. Call me baby baby love the nipples, turn to a giant when I slide in the middle, find the answers to the riddles. Never light like feather, whether you prefer to change positions unpredictable weather. Stretch the stretch need rubber, magical like a genie when I rub her, narrow journey produce stutter, long distance make me tougher.

 It will workout have us working out, legs on shoulder auto float, get you wet water splashing on the side of a boat. Physique from back wonderful figure, you bad someone who miss jail after pulling the trigger, when you call I come of course you come quicker. Workout let's exercise love, block the world out new word sexcercise love. Even if its a dream I will wake up sweating, imagine a trance have you guessing, it's right that I will keep you fly never left wing.

Roland S Brown

<u>**Wish You Could Read My Mind**</u>

Attempting to find a lady like is you is like searching for snow in summertime wish you could read my mind. My feelings for you transcend daily we can call this lover time wish you could read my mind. My heart reach out for your passionate romance, you are the type of lady who make a guy try to put rings on both hands wish you could read my mind.

If i was to get a dollar for everytime i think about you, i would be rich wish you could read my mind. Tick tock tick tock forget the clock tick tock, tick tock let the watch watch the clock hands clap woow!! Mamacita you drive me crazy no turn back now wish you could read my mind.Have an idea of crazy when i think about you wish you could read my mind. Gold line, gold mine gold fine gold shine wish you could read my mind.

Your physique let me mesmerize, wife qualities display in your eyes. God know this feelings is true i wont emphasize wish you could read my mind. When i see you stop staring please i have to beg my eyes, that was a joke voila!! Hope it make you happy for me to care for you is my karma wish you could read my mind.

Even if you are like the Halley comet that appears every decade, am thankful that i know you my thoughts enslave wish you could read my mind. There is always a soft soft spot for you in my heart wish you could read my mind.The cupid arrow dart like darts, this feelings impress me from the start wish you could read my mind. No wonder the word start is similar to tart because that was the sweetest time for my heart wish you could read my mind. C'est la vie mon ami you never could read my mind. Sadly I finish with these hopeful lines wish you could read my mind, wish you could read my mind.

By: Roland S Brown

We Put The Mental Shackles On

When you clutch instruments that bring pain create loud sound bang!! Bang!! In vain you destroys the same blood that runs through your veins you put the mental shackles on. The old lady on the roadside, hunger display on her mouth side, you just focusing on a boat ride. Poisonous copper inside shining golden gold glitter outside, you put the mental shackles on. Poison dripping from your fang old cobra injecting doubtful doubt in minds, we need more Martin Luther rewind the time. Nowadays vanity design the shine, by any means necessary we resign the lines you put the mental shackles on.

Learn from the past live for the future and present, love your heritage receive the blessings the open presents. Cultural dance no stress in your presence, out of many one people this message is heaven sent. Disrespect heritage the evidence good deeds hardly become eminent, you put the mental shackles on. Let's forget the colour of our skin, we bleed the same blood, we all need the same love. Cleanse your mind else its the same grudge, we deny our feelings its not every time we need game love, you put the mental shackles on.

We will never create a perfect world, working together we can create a better world. Make an attempt to heal broken wings, less fight to reign this only let our people fall like dropping drizzling rain. Soak in painful pain, mental shackles no clinking clanking of chains, you put the mental shackles on. We put the mental shackles on once , we put the mental shackles on twice, thrice even by choice. The past is the past free your minds and learn from the sign of the signs, then we will have golden minds. Bury gold in a mine, discover yourself create your shine, please take the mental shackles off.

Roland S Brown

We Are Not Able We Are Not Abel

Label as curse sons of Adam ignore wisdom, label as hell bound no place in the kingdom, we are not sons of Abel. Learn to hide love, survive inside grudge, forgive and ignite love we are not able. Its hard to forgive and forget, everyone see our type as target we are not Abel. We fight with might we learn the hard way, pick a Queen a day , the deck of card way, love one person let the hearty heart stay we are not able. We should learn to balance our imperfections, instead of fighting losing battles for perfection, difficult to understand our generation, aim to discover meaningless intentions we are not Abel. Its not right to steal, find it in your mind attempt to forgive the man that steal, picture famine fanning family without meal, mother yawning hunger saying bad morning that's steel we are not Abel.

Working for a minimum wage, mentally we still live as slave, talents have no boundaries release it from the cage we are not able. The system make us victims circumstances of life, we get little privilege to make choices, pain slice our heart and we never create knives we are not Abel. Fortunate if we live to walk with a cane, when your close brother might be Cain, forgive us God we are not able, forgive us God we are not Abel. Get inspire by this two hundred and ninety four words, folks throw curse at us with Bible verse. The poisonous words from the mouth your curse, it continue the next generation will hear when our souls disappear in the air the same words we are not able we are not Abel.

By: Roland S Brown

<u>**There Use To Be A Time, There Will Be A Time, The Current Time**</u>

There use to be a time brothers and sisters enhance shine, there will be a time the current time shock your mind, no tick tock when the clock strike nine. There use to be a time which let me hate the current time, carefree free minds competitions which tree you climb. There use use to be a time words of motivation to climb, there will be a time individuals motivate elevate your mind,the current time words attempt to block the shining shine, burning words imagine cuts meet lime. Blossoms bloom like may in May, autumn fall determination pave the way, cruelty of the world judging judgements make a million today, still cannot save the day.

There use to be a time only age let us see nine, brothers age sixteen still feel nine, let you stop when you don't see sign the current time. There use to be a time we wear one shoes nothing to lose, the current time the clothes the shoes we choose might make the news, choosing friends turn foe confuse. We know we got enemies, enemies envy empty, friendship sink vessels empty, life short only cricket give a chance at a century. There use to be a time, there will be a time, the current time the current time, shocking news the current time.

Roland S Brown

The Way Of The World

Visualize the sad dark empty look in the human eyes, just the remain of human qualities in disguise, take a few seconds analyze great deeds that fade away from the mind, its hard to be kind when most is unkind, be careful of mankind. Smiles display bare fangs, snakes that learn to walk on concrete, ravens that can speak, above ground demons with no leash. The way of the world enlighten me that love might ruin my heart caring will let me fragile, increase our beast instincts thoughts real agile, few times I picture myself in a pile, bodies everywhere, I care attitude never care, altitude anywhere, gratitude never near.

We never show any weakness until its late the precious word caring we misplace, nice people hardly fit in with this place, wonder if am from somewhere else just displace. I atone for my sins, my only option is to win, before you hardly notice my presence gone like the wind. We are able to endure hardship, success the hardest target, wish we could purchase it at the market. Need positive movements search deep inside the mind stumbling to find light, the fight struggling to find the might in the darkness, new human competition which heart is the darkest.

We hardly can put even the truth in words without doubt and weakness in the eyes, we surrender ourselves to Instincts inside just to survive, look at the way we survive and continue to believe, we lose more energy if we continue to deceive. The way of the world and circumstances decide the shape of our hearts, born in the dark we stumble just to see a spark, love and hate never stay apart, the way of the world it live in our hearts.

Roland S Brown

Support

We all need support when the weight pressure the shoulder, your thoughts will deceive you thinking support is necessary when you are senile feeling older, challenge obstacles together removing the negative boulders. No man is an Island no man stand alone, my brain have the ideas yet I did not create the phone. The phone that I am presently holding, a next man create it so I can attempt to make my plans golden. The first step we make we get help, it was someone who teach us to buckle our belts, someone teach us to eat ice cream before it melt. Observe the time technological in its prime, the gadgets need electricity to operate on time. Obtain internet you need telephone lines, flow that through your mind, we all need each other to climb. Motivate someone today, you might direct them to a better way, avoid letting the negative words easier to say. Never use extra strength motivate a person already flying, just nodding your head will motivate the person trying. A flying person at a new altitude, struggling person mislead gratitude, share kind words everyone need motivational attributes.

Your support encourage me, the greatest gift I get for free, no bribery still you support me, genuine than money that bring jealous in relationship with envy. I Would thank everyone individually if I have the time, instead I write these lines. Read between these lines, even if you get 363 rainy days never give up the someday the sun will shine, no complaining use the energy to appreciate the time.

Roland S Brown

The Gentleman Meet The Sex Goddess: The Other Side

The gentleman side realize there are times when I still wish you were mine mine, in a state were I see the bright light but am still blind blind. Our angelic heart use to beat rapidly the same pace, just seeing you use to run my pain away no race. Sex Goddess I never write a love poem to make it rhyme, when I think about you my mind go back in time, leave my thoughts flying. Cliché you were like magnet am like steel touché the way you make me feel. My love use to Rush Shae, you were my baby baby even though I never need to hush Shae.

Words can never explain, you might think I feel no pain, its just faith let me escape insane when your love runaway like a train. This is life I just hope you find someone worthy, consider your happiness even if it hurt me. That's how I care about you, you will always live in my thoughts even when I find someone new TRUE.

My other side let me vision your breasts fit just for my mouth, everytime we touch is like I feel my soul coming out. Boobies trap your qualities glory overload no holding back, greenlight when am on the go no holding back. Holding your sexy body in my arms, leave my heart on fire my entire body warm. When I touch the tip of your nipples I feel your nipples vibrating, before I slip inside your pride slippery ice skating. Remember the first time when we do it, feel like a hand between your leg grip the wet pool stick. I call and you come, you call and I come, still feel real even though we use a......sssssshh.

I still remember the missionary mission, you look in my eyes tell me not to change position that's visionary vision. I fight to satisfy you and not explode, inside you feel like heaven on earth maybe more, inside outside you have the worth. Your pride always feel brand new, words useless you don't have a single clue. Mesmerizing feeling that let me know I love you, Sex Goddess you great but I think past sex when it come to you. You are great in every way, use to just wish you were in my arms everyday. Our feelings is the storm that will clear the way, come collect my love just like your pay, bet this poem let you smile at the words I say. Come brighten my life need to know the difference between night and day, that would make my day, thinking of you makes my day today.

Roland S Brown

Success Scorch Snake

Jealousy let you find strength to discriminate, no strength to motivate, still you wishing on heaven gate. Success scorch the earth show the snakes, people jealous for nothing you don't own the cake, eyes of a Jezebel I feel the fake, qualities of a false Malachi messenger prophetic snake. Even smoke rising burn your eyes daily, you demonstrate jealousy for a playful baby, your thoughts modern day slavery. Snake on concrete scorch concrete watch serpent sizzle, you want the world to revolve once you are the middle, pagans in disguise praising Satan hallelujah belittle. Praying God give you blessing in shower, praying blessing drizzle for your neighbour no power.

Hate have no colour black white, it develop in the mind when positivity take a flight, jealousy envy stay alike, even day make way for a darker night, find success if you want a fight. Lying lips an abomination to the Lord Proverbs, who act faithfully his delights wonderful words. Your tongue plot deception part of the Psalms, like a sharp razor worker of deceit your faith reborn. Jamaican slang we say badmind, you would change if jealousy was a landmine, fight all you want it's final cannot change God time.

Roland S

Brown

Raindrops

Take a second meditate when you see raindrops, the rain bring pain like tear drops, have you wishing the pain stop, wishing pain was gone when the rain stop. Loneliness clutching for happiness like baby stretching for a hug, good times bad times let us appreciate the love. The rain teach us to enjoy the sunshine, the sunshine teach us to balance the rain time, we cannot change time, richness poverty same time. The raindrops show us equality power of the shower, everyone can get wet even if we try to cover, this life is not our neither the hour.

Think positive the rain disrupt your plans for a greater way, after rainfall sunshine brighter day, life journey teach the fighter way. Raindrops close my eyes the splashing I analyze, glorious to be living I realize, if life was selling you don't of to state a price for the prize, just by living we still pay the price. Enjoy the weather its a treasure, even when obstacles bring pressure, even when death digging at the treasure, remember we never prove if the dead see any weather.

Roland S Brown

The Sting Of The Scorpio Scorpion Miss November

Miss November you I will always remember, you let me fall in love my mind merry like festive December, no competition when you let me enter. Sexiness plus your lips, God give me the greatest gifts. Focus eyes Miss November I admire, your appearance shock me no wire, intoxicated burning desire, we a perfect match no fire. Blessing Scorpio Miss November in November, when you leave believe I miss November, even though you are the reason I do not want to miss November. Born in the winter time, manage to still be fiery than summer time. Blame me when you feel tiresome because you are running on my mind, exciting when I think about you like am hunting for a mine, words cannot describe personality one of a kind.

Brighten my day like the sunshine, its a blessing to know you exist like the sunshine, I love you like a leprechaun love gold coin. Enjoy this month because it yours, receive blessings abundant sand to seashore, November rush your loving I need more. 8 days and 10 hours leave, then your birthday will roll up like a sleeve, 21 times the charm that's a blessing indeed, have a marvelous birthday as you proceed. January February March April May, June July August September fade a way, October next November my better day, Miss November don't miss November you pave the way, just to make December a merry better way.

Roland S Brown

Me , Myself And I Me

Me the personality that's killing me slowly like ME, characteristics of myself, fret not thyself avoid high shelves thoughts aim tall tree. I the personality that will reply, love who love me believe me I try, poor or rich get caskets no one transcend to the sky, still willing to stay faithful look to the sky. Respect the creator of life humans on earth want praise I dont see any of them in the sky, we equal from we use the same oxygen someday we will die, precious life just walk by, just a next poor soul telling the world goodbye. When there is hardly any good in goodbye, unless we tell goodbye goodbye. Me myself and I hardly can remember the last time I cry, broken wings the price I pay high fly, hope I did not tell the real ones bye-bye. Pain design the way of the heart, nowadays I realize i must analyze the way I talk, turn victim of the system the way we walk.

I confidently love myself daily, smokey room everywhere crawl away baby, something that they say hurt me daily, still I find pleasure like kissing a lady. Me myself and I ambitions aiming to the sky high, instruments that get me high, thoughts infuse with smoke climbing to the sky, when am up there high wish i could tell God hi. Me myself and I if I encounter pain its me alone, if money control most people why do we need a crown. Its me myself and I, look at the way we lie, we text someone special dying for a reply, staring at the phone might develop blurry eyes. Journey of life might turn an idol with a killer instinct, brothers all for themselves receive praises because we clip wings, killing a brother still make you a victim. Better him than me some of us will say, its a suicidal future imagine the price we pay, just remember we all of to pay, some just pay sooner less privilege before they cast away. Me myself and I claim I don't need love, lonely time still let me desire hugs, only God can save us new version of the great flood.

Roland S Brown

<h1 style="text-align:center"><u>Masks</u></h1>

Which mask did you wear today? The mask desiring a better pay, ooooohhh!!!! The mask that pretend pain fade away. Which mask did you wear today? The silver Judas mask pretending you love your neighbours, the mask wishing your enemies tear like paper. Deadly serpent eyes, Delilah in disguise, using forbidden fruit to make a pie. Which mask did you wear today? The smile after you just cheat on your wife, the acrimony piercing heart like a knife, the darkness taking over the light. Mask of deceptive disguise, mask of not appreciating life, making sins pleasure by choice, reluctantly you write the right. Easy choice you left the right, mask of confusion left thinking right. Which mask did you wear today? The mask acting like you love humanity, tell me do you feel that warmth when you hug vanity?

The mask of thinking before you answer, mask of weak thoughts devilish sponsor, before you answer. Did you wear the mask, that hide your past, breaking the masks of apprentice in your class, that's how you hide your past. Which mask did you wear today? Pretend that you happy for someone success, someone glory story killing you inside you upset, balance the universe never object. Did you wear the mask like guns hands aiming at pockets, venom dripping from fatal fangs like faucet, spiritual blood sucking your asset. Wearing the mask denying yourself you keep it real, designing yourself to church you bring a steel. Find hungry mouth bring a meal, even when you know one good deed cannot seal the deal. Which mask did you wear today? Smoke of hell still on your clothes, happy with your family other family bringing rose. Pretending to promote life you watering rose, pathetic thinking you change your ways when you change your clothes.

Mask on of saying we love, saying we trust, still making love using glove. Master masking mask we might be modern animals, human have canines greed for cook meat undercover cannibals, just check the food chain it's our animal instincts eating animals. Masks everywhere advance vampire draining energy, leaving an empty vessel in the cemetery. Masks conceal hell in love not the letter L, place we call earth hell of hell. Which mask you wear today? If you read this poem that line, echo through mind, am just the messenger now await the signs.

By: Roland S Brown

Love Nihilism

Picture the crimson heavenly body vanishing into the light of dawn, in the blink of an eye you were gone, we use to hold hands through the raging storms. We put on masks of lies and throw what we believe in the darkness like prey trap, our bright futures turn fade black. Distance between us is earth and heaven we look to the sky, place of haven memories live in the mind. With longing tragedies repeating inside, I laugh at times to ease my pain, win-lose memories I regain the disdain pain again. Pain in vain my veins like ferocious winds, wind vane direct my aching heart to pain. Here in the dark my smile turn to frown, hardly could find reasonable reasons to be king without you no throne.

Our endless pain have no outlets, we bring heartbreak at each other doorsteps. I drench your heart in precious desire colour crimson red, we swear no lies eventually we lie in bed, we lie in bed. There is no past to look back on, since we let feelings move on, I keep telling myself the entire time, love need assistance we both do the entire climb. I think I would have nothing to lose anymore, like the shinning moon I drift through the silence, self love can shine light on any darkness. I will utilize the strength of the light in the future I am building immortal dreams, me myself and I a unique mortal team.

The self love inside me, keep me alive, when my heart get sting from the Queen of the beehive. Even pain with sorrow now drive me onward, I may break my neck if I look backward. On the path of my salvation, passion fuel me, guide me toward my true destiny, learn to control my feelings, a few might envy me. If it was not love we feel it was close, my heart use to skip a beat even when you keep on your clothes. My heart feels like the garden first time you bring a rose, now we disgust each other imagine seeing a human face without a nose. I still imagines both of us staring at shooting stars, wishing we become each other shining star. You are always my shining star so shine, you still glitter like gold goals golden gold mine. My eyes desire keep in the healthy living mind, even gold someday will vanish from the mines and absolutely the precious mind.

Roland S Brown

Kevin Poetry Competition: Poetic Poem

People!! People!! People!! Welcome to the Kevin All Poetry competition, to win every poet mission, even when we have the same eyes different visions, different submission. Submit a poem at least vaguely relating to the theme, oh my God finding words become harder it seem. When I think about 50 dollars I remember my boot heel lean, plus I can change meal less rice and sardine. The challenge request poetry about specific people, specific people revving brains like old vehicle. This competition leave poets minds feeble, confusion piercing poets brains like sharp needles. Kevin All Poetry competition require poetic poet to write about this tree, not the trees, finding words burn thoughts like CD, rhymes turn on and off like TV. Please don't be hurt if Kevin poetry miss your poem, there is a lot of poems, just wear your glory close to your heart like an emblem. Kevin All Poetry competition will make suggestions about your work, just keep writing poem your journey is steady no jerks, don't let your minds mislead you competition competing complete jerks, possibilities poets continue the work.

Comments might hurt, remember the precious green plants come from this earth, believe in yourself this poetry competition display your worth. Show don't tell they say, avoid emotional word play, avoid forcing your rhymes, to be honest we all do sometime. Kevin poetry competition enlighten us to avoid cliché, we are poets if the sky is falling we say it in a neat way, poet will say the earth soon kiss the sky cliché. Gold winners 6 months stay out, don't let talents talent go south, better you mention our names in your gold mouth, golden motivation bring the gold out. Enter Kevin poetry contest, not to be the best, not to prove with rhymes you bulletproof vest, enter the competition poets with a passionate interest.

By: Roland S Brown

Invisible Chains: Limited Freedom

The bird In the cage reminder of our past, we just blind we still live in the dark, it is just time hide the thoughts. Chains still bind our feet, the mind hope to do greatness, the feet still hesitate to make a start lateness. Nowadays even smiles are fake, a shower of faith, try to correct our mistake. Cherish life we are not here by mistake, crawling on your knees before you fly is no disgrace. False tongues is a new trend love is not blind look at life, sisters and brothers look at life, perilous journey visualize the book of life. Someone lie to me daily I stay humble knowing I might do the same, yet still my heart feel the pain. The heart is a wild fire who dare to tame, consequences of life burn us before we see the flame. Even kisses don't feel the same, feel like an instrument for causing pain.Still we fight cause we might break the chains, see the light break the pain.

We are still chain mentally, bind your mind fatally. Give yourself a hug, you climb with chains on your feet, show yourself some love make yourself complete. Visions getting clear, missions getting clearer, hold my hands saviour, your love is greater than the paper, you stay around when everyone disappear like vapour. I always feel your spirit you fight with me to the finish, without you saviour my life is finish. We try to steer our life, still in the destine destination, sins we never resist the temptation, struggle twist the motivation. Still some of us rise and some fall, this is life God motivate the blind ones with a miss call.

Roland S Brown

Idea Of Pain

We never know how someone feel we just have an idea we share the
sorrow, minds get empty heart deadly hollow. Pain let you know you are
alive might see tomorrow, hoping for less sorrow, for the life we borrow.
Life might look invaluable when you have it, not to the persons who see it
vanish like magic. Even when you hate life you wish to live longer, when
you live longer you wish you were stronger. I am force to believe I
conquer anger, head barely above water anchor under. Pain is knowing
you care yet no one believe, time turn to ashes shorten life like short
sleeve, pain is running from love heartless athlete. Life is a vehicle we
watch from the backseat, an unpredictable journey solid concrete. Life
create pain when someone soul crash bones turn to ash, once you alive
automatically force to watch.

A face that use to make you smile lost, get us cross feel we have an idea of carrying the cross. We still feel the presence of someone we lose, pain keeping it a secret before society description of you confuse. I know pain equal sorrows bring weakness to the feet, travel upward to achieve defeat. It reach the mind the true master, few seconds later eye water. Attempting to drown the disaster that will wake us in the night, we are not too weak we put up a fight. Against the unknown, picture a body without a backbone, icy heart on lock down. Thanks for pain let us know we alive, even when it feel like it pierce our heart on the inside. It bring pain when we stop feeling pain, when we mediate only lifeless vessel remain. Even at birth we bring the pain, we only have an idea everyone will never feel the same.

By: Roland S Brown

<u>Guh Weh Jealousy Yuh Bad Mine</u>

Yuuh tek yuh moutamatic offa repeat, yuh beak a guh longa likkle parakeet, seh yuh seet and yuh nuh seet, seh lime sweet and it nuh sweet. Anuh 32 teet yuh luv chat wid yuh 64 teet, mout cyah res else fi yuh own wuda weak. Tel lie bout people a get hol dung wid obeah, yuh mout a di obeah, yuh belly big mussi a drink people bizniz lacka soda, sprinkle false news lacka powda, yuh mout a rotten naw talk di oda. Yuh bad mine shuda be yuh miggle name, yuh mine bad red eye fi fame, yuh radio mout tun on all dawg shame, suppose sumady jus cum from toilit dem name sssshhhhaaamme, tell mi a suh yuh wuda call dem name. Yuh wuss dan jan kro dem only nyam dead meat, a just dat dem affi eat, yuh nuh reject nuttin offa yuh head top mussi toilit seat. Wah di mouta massi issue, yuh mout su staat roll toilit tissue. Spit a fly people wah bline wen yuh a chat mussi mout ninja, God mek di poor gal yuh seh har toe luk lacka ginja, hear she almos tel yuh fi S yuh mada big finga, dedly shawp wud yuh use dem haamful lacka splinta.

Slow dung lock yuh mout Bolt sprinta, a race yuh race fi guh tel summa lie bout winta, guh seh dem bwoy tief out di man ginja. Yuh lie wid lie more lie bawn, yuh fambilly a wah cahtigerry 5 hurrimout staam, tell lie pon all baby befo dem bawn, alrite fat fowl gwaan guh pic up caan. Yuh lova kiss people biz di way gossip stay pon yuh lips, cyah kip nuttin ol fridge weh a drip, tek dis guh chat yuh flop weh a flip, guh chat bout Mista Dick. Nuh matta how yuh bad mine people stil a climb, duh a new design fi yuh dutty mind, guh washie heng it out pon line. Bet dat free yuh dutty mine, bet yuh cyah stop chat flip a coin, try elevaat guh flip a mine.

Roland S

Brown

Goat Mout

Goat mout tek people bizniz outta yuh mout, luk yah bleatin wen yuh a shout, stil hungry fi people bizniz all wen yuh hav a ful mout. Rotating goat mout always a move, yuh anuh news reporta stil a run dung clues, nuh baddi nuh fit inna fi yuh shoes, all if yuh hav di worl yuh stil a lose. Wi use yuh mout fi nuh mek people rise, nuh plantain nuh fit lacka yuh mout di way dat x-ahsize, yuh same yapping mout wi en up tek a life. Ebrybody affi chat wi kno dat, anuh han wen fi yuh mout a clap, set pon spring affi ketch a rat, only cheese yuh mout need fi be a rat trap. Yuh hav bizniz as wel memba dat, watch di po ol woman pot, wid yuh goat mout talk seh it blak, lata di po woman cyah fine har pot.

Yuh fling yuh goat mout pon di man crop a yam, wen him si yuh luk pon yuh lacka how sum rasta luk pon a ham, lo people bizniz betta unda stan fi ova stan, falla people bizniz di madman almos chop off yuh han. Yuh a

maay everytime inna di year, a baay people bizniz soon drop out yuh hair.
Wonda if yuh bawn May a maay June yuh lie like July, ebry likkle ting yuh
readi fi cry, mi naw supprize if yuh did help get Jesus crucify. Goat mout
ebryting yuh talk bout tun poison faas, mek sum tings pass si if people nuh
prospa faas, sumady su tell yuh bout yuh rrraa class, nuttin naw guh stitch
wen yuh haa a claat.

Roland S Brown

<u>Baby S.I.N(Survival Instincts Naturally)</u>

From birth we see light as sinners, vanity control us we fight we cannot all be winners, Queens with curse wombs born killers. Surely we are sinful at birth, sinful from before our baby feet touch earth, producer of life next step in curse, wish we could get cure by bible verse. From the wombs the wicked spread lies, flashbacks wondering about the time I encounter lies, violence we see better close the right deny the left eye, high thoughtful thinking I see heaven when I step high. Wash your hands deny yourself, leave blood still boiling thoughts that melt, you below soul escape air vent. Nature deserving of wrath there is no one righteous not even one, ask the Romans study the journey of Christianity you understand. The bible state we will receive death due to sin, drop it the humans who think they got wings. Remember David carry a sling, noteworthy title of a King, the legacy continue that's why we try to win.

This is life we were born in sin, where is hell it depends on who is asking, imagine producing curse offsprings. Matthew state in the end, we have a chance to enter heaven if we become children, this is difficult when life get intense. Ask us not to be like children when it come to evil, words telling us to be like infants in evil, think mature dark prefer light people still threading the needles. Accepting the past, mirror mirror break the glass, attempt to do better that's the task, be a student and a teacher you will top the class.

Roland S Brown

MY MOTIVATION

You are my motivation, you enlighten my mind, God Godly creation I see the signs. You let me daydream still you let me stay focus, our connection remain robust. I see the wife qualities clearly when I look into your eyes, it COUNT when you look into my eyes, you are a blessing in disguise, in my visions it's you I vividly visualize. You are special I show it with poetry, now my heart feel the glory of the story, it is a win-win situation even if you ignore me.

I cannot imagine living in a world without you, without you by my side it's like am living in a world without you. I don't want your heart only want you to be there for me, you are the light now I see my journey clearly. Life is no fairy tale am not Prince charming saving a Princess, my title prevail Legendary darling I never try to impress, worthy time yes I will invest, call me COUNT I choose you to be my COUNTESS.

R.S Brown

<u>Amazon Online Magic</u>

Magical online multinational technological company Amazon, individuals
focusing on e-commerce cloud computing Amazon have a plan, artificial
intelligence no guessing you choose number one. Thanks to Amazon
create a career for Roland, talented Author Fiery talent from a infamous
land, KDP self publish privilege to design your own brand, we all need
assistance believe me Amazon understand. Base in Seattle formerly
Cadabra Inc the rising computing battle, this is life even giants sometime

get tackle, life is never easy like picking an apple, however it's possible to achieve the impossible ask Apple, New York New York the big apple, Amazon Amazon find Washington DC you find Seattle.

 Amazon gift the big tech company along with Google Apple and Facebook, Rolandauthor.blogspot.com Amazon give Author page a welcome to my place look. You can visit Amazon Author central, KDP community meet new pen pal, Kindle Owner's Lending library close to book rental. Educational programming on the internet give kids a push, Audible studio downloadable audio books, music that steal your soul musical crook.

 s reading The Fiery Eye Beast Rolling Calf by Roland, non readers still need to checkout Amazon, Peruvian Columbian Ecuadorian Venezuelan Brazilian, you are welcome to check if Amazon flow like river Amazon. Ignite the world from July 1994 to 1995 present Amazon still manage to stay strong, provision of more jobs on the land, respect every South American that visit their Amazon, forget geographical location, less barriers to visit the American Amazon. Joyful Joy joyous qualities Amazon never Omit, find happiness grab your digital DC Comics. Amazon Prime delivery on Sunday, you are wonderful have a wonderful day, you can open your package before Monday, want a Nike just do it by Tuesday.

 Festive season purchase toys and games , your kids will love you more Amazon provide a reason warmth by flame, cold time seek comfort with burning flames, shipping of alcohol heat in your cold body ease the pain. Check Amazon Amazon whether you old or in your prime, keep shopping online, Amazon go the extra mile for customers no stop sign, those lines so true put it on rewind. Delivery for customers in the cold, Amazon create a way to create warm in your soul. Summer winter respect for customer still the same, just order online Amazon employees care they will bare the pain, think Amazon everytime you see a plane. Any products or service you want Amazon may have it, appear at your doorstep call that Amazon magic, quality service for customers that's a habit, Amazon will deliver carrots even if the order is from a rabbit, thanks to Amazon giving customers the privilege of online magic.

Roland S Brown

The Two Edged Sword

The two edged sword is full of deceit, can I ask you a question please? That's a question just get release, most person say that before a next question flow with the breeze, without realizing we just create self deceit. Another deception of the tongue say we will be there in a minute, have someone waiting in the cold that's frigid, the two edged sword have no limit. I swear if you touch my phone I will kill you!!! The world would be empty if everytime we express that cliché with truth, two edged sword get loose small feet big shoes, we listen words carefully one word still leave us with twist news. Hands up who talk hundred percent truth??? Lies attach to tongues like guitar strings musical lies we play tune deceptive flute, we hear a news the way we talk it display we hold the camera and say shoot.

Hebrew 4 verse 11 give details about the two edged sword, just careful how you use it will break your bones fragile board, careful of the two edged sword, Kings use it to influence Knights to use sword. The two edged sword always stay active, it can be water in your mouth get release it become acid, wonder if our words can be the reason in the morning breath smell rancid.

The deceiving tongue a fretwork in flesh designing degrading fretful fret, the deadly poisonous viper create this way no fretsaw forget fingerboard when we play this fret. Self claim Seraphim serenade of lies to a lover, hope the feelings remain the same after you leave from under the cover. Words is not just words the two edged sword give it power, the words we use maybe it is our mouth that need shower, the mind or the tongue you decide which weapon deception is lower.

Roland S Brown

<u>GET WELL SOON MY FRIEND(Dedication To A Friend That Was ill)</u>

When pain make us a victim, let us realize good times everything we missing, painful pain delicate body twisting, the burdens on our shoulders haunting heavy lifting. No human should exist to feel pain, that thought is in vain, once blood run through your vein.

Pain will attempt to drive you insane, break you physically window pane,
break you mentally pain in pain. Hope is there in this poem I send, it's a
blessing you are able to read this to the end, this is life hope you get
better soon my friend.

Roland S Brown

Lies we tell ourselves

Imagine the lies we tell ourselves we don't need anyone help, even when you buy still get by handouts to claim what's on the shelves, be the great person you claim to be create it yourself. We receive assistance the moment we were born look at the lies we tell ourselves, someday the truth will beat us like a belt, if we make it be a baby again lie on our bed. The lies we tell ourselves that below earth is hell, our mind might be slow snail in a shell, hello hell is in our mind, the deeds we design display the signs. How many will lead a old person that is blind, you see physically in your mind mentally you are blind, unkind your kind will not give the poor beggar a coin. Lie we tell ourselves that love is blind, look at life that's love we will see the sign, its a blessing even to read this line, congrats you are alive. Your brain is minute to think a minute is nothing, consider that precious you can lose life in a second when death hunting.

Lies we tell ourselves when our mood down, that we are not Kings and Queens if we don't wear a crown, oxygen that give life should be wearing the crown, we are all equal no matter who in the town sit on a throne. Lies we tell ourselves life is money with abundant assets, we are equal cut yourself red blood dripping no water from a faucet, money root of all evil skeleton in the closets. Lies we tell ourselves the price don't matter when we wage war, some person will love it imagine the ice on a fake star, war will always be a reminder similar to face scar. We will keep telling ourselves lies, blind to life the blessing in disguise, open your eyes before it's too late to realize.

Roland S Brown

Gayle Town District,

Borobridge P.O.,

St. Ann

December 10, 2019.

No Name

Dear Reviewer,

Determine, stoical, hardworking and calm in my sight are the qualities that characterize me the Author of The Fiery Eye Beast: Rolling Calf. I am from a small farming community name Gayle Town geographical location is Jamaica in the West Indies. My visionary writing career start from poetry in high school, I would write a poem for a girl I admire. This enhance my poetry skill as an upcoming poet I have poem in my local language patois, English translation is available. Writing stories about my surroundings become a part of my journal, if I have a wonderful day at the river as I touch my book it become a next story. I did not get the privilege to fully educate myself but my determination is my weapon that I utilize to conquer those educational boundaries. I am self employ farming and other activities I also work as a security at a primary school protecting kids.

My inspiration for my movie script/book start from an idea that I experience myself. We grow up hearing traditions of Rolling Calf a mythical creature. This tradition live in our mind, I was walking with a friend one late night. We hear sound signifying things we hear in the tradition clanking chains. We were just teenagers we attempt to identify what was causing the sound before we move. It was a clear area we see nothing so we run he hold on to my shirt I could not leave him. I did not see the creature itself but even as an adult writing this I can still feel the presence of that night. A feelings telling you that something bad will happen if you don't run. I still see that person on a regular basis Triston Johnson even when we joke about the way he grab my shirt to make sure I don't escape and leave him. We always admit there was a evil presence that night running was the best option. My movie script/book is base mostly on reality events that take place in my community some before I was born. Anyone get the privilege to talk to an individual from these local communities Gayle Town, Long Bough, Morgan Forest they can relate. Mention the Rolling Calf to even a teenager in Jamaica they will tell you the tale of The Fiery Eye Beast: Rolling Calf.

120

Yours truly,

Roland Serlington Brown